CRINGETASTIC CONTENT
UNCENSORED

by

Matthew Barron

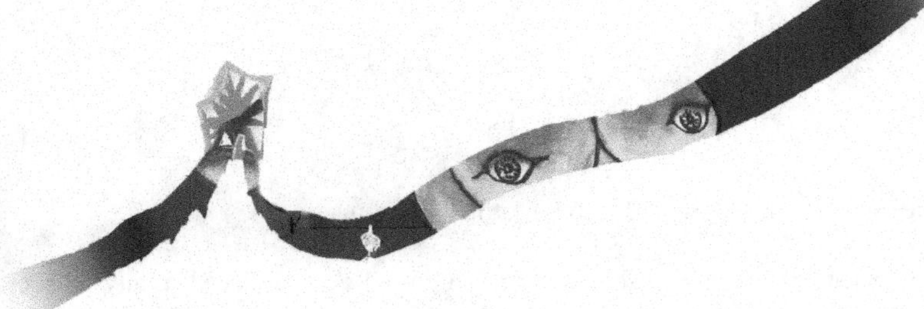

Published by
Submatter Press

ISBN: 978-1-954482-07-4 (paperback)
eISBN: 978-1-954482-08-1 (eBook)

For more information, to contact the author, or to order additional books, visit:
submatterpress.com

TABLE OF CONTENTS

LOVE BOT LB65244

Originally published in *Roboterotica: 23 Electric Tales of Erotica* from Pill Hill Press April 3, 2012

I tried to ignore the grimy tile floor and concentrated on the throbbing pussy surrounding my cock. It was *real.*

"Oh Yes," came the recorded voice. "That's it. That's the way."

I ran my hand along the hard plastic vibrating underneath me, found the fleshy breasts. I squeezed, pinching the hardening nipples between my fingers. They were real too.

"You're so good. That's the spot. Right there."

It was good. I almost forgot where I was, kissed her open mouth, but I stopped myself. Framed by pink synthetic hair, her permanently rounded mouth had been the receptacle of things I didn't want to think about. You could save credits by sharing a two-fer.

The recorded voice broke in again, but my penis had softened. I closed my eyes and moved the shoulder armature, positioning the hand over my ass. That was real.

She throbbed, oozing over my cock, and I stiffened. I could imagine the slick puddle of her juice underneath my balls. The pussy tightened and pulsed, milking me as I rocked back and forth over the plastic shell.

"That's the way," she said. "No one does it like you. You're the best."

I could feel myself throbbing inside her. It was too late to stop.

"That's it. Don't stop. Almost there. Almost..."

Suddenly, everything went dead. Her temperature became cold, and her slickness was now a sticky glue. It was like pumping a jar of molasses.

"Please deposit 25 credits."

I groaned with frustration and slapped the hard plastic shell under me. My dick still throbbed inside her, but her pussy was useless, even painful to try and fuck. I grabbed my pants from the tile floor beside us, searched though the pockets, but found my credits lacking. I pulled out with a groan. Her pussy and thighs were real, nothing below the knees. These truck stop models only had the bare essentials. My cock bobbed with my pulse, the thick veins pulsing. I had been so close.

Glued to the love bot's plastic bean chassis, her breasts had tiny freckles and a bruise where someone had gotten too rough. I grabbed the cold things, squeezed, rolled the flat nipple between my fingers. Then I grabbed myself. What else could I do? What a waste of credits.

The stall door kicked in. I grabbed my pants, but gloved hands lifted me from the floor before I could put them on.

A woman in a SWAT uniform leaned over the love-bot, examined her breasts and thighs. "It's her."

Her partner, I couldn't tell much about him under the black helmet, turned the bot over. "It's not her."

The woman took off her helmet, ran her finger along the engraved serial number, then examined a photograph. "But it has to be; the freckle pattern..."

"It's not her, Lebronski," her partner insisted.

They quickly took fingerprints from the bot, then left the stall. The woman, Lebronski, gave me a glance on her way out, and I covered my crotch with my hands. She had short, red hair, and a sinewy neck. She was strong, the kind of woman I had always wanted to date, but never could. A woman like that had no use for a man like me.

"What do we do about the pervert?" she asked her partner.

"He hasn't broken any laws," he said.

They were at the door before I finally spoke. "Wait! What was this all about?"

Lebronski turned to me with sarcastic concern. "Oh, so sorry. Did we ruin your 15 minutes?" She tossed a couple cards on the floor. "Have another, my compliments."

"No," I said. "I'm not interested in credits." I was, actually, but she didn't need to know that. "Was she stolen or something?"

Her mouth creased. "Stolen? You could say that. You pervs never like to think where the human parts come from for those love bots, don't like to be called necrophiliacs." She turned without another word, and the door swung shut behind her.

I bent over to pick up the credits and saw the love bot's ass facing me, her real, and very lifeless ass.

* * *

Lebronski met me in the police waiting room. "They said you wanted to see me?"

She didn't recognize me with my pants on. I couldn't decide if that was good or bad. I didn't want her to look at me like she had yesterday afternoon, but I also didn't want to explain who I was. Without the bulky, black body armor, I could see more of her figure under her blue shirt. Her arms were lean, tone, and I could imagine the rest of her was much the same, like steel, harder than any love bot.

"Well?" she said.

"I wanted to try and help." I paused awkwardly.

There was a spark in her hazel eyes. "You." She looked around the waiting area and walked back behind the reception desk. Without looking back, she said, "Come to my office."

I hurried to catch up, and she shut her office door behind us. Her office was neat, orderly, everything in its place. There were no personal items to give it any character of its own. I sat across from her at her desk.

"A young girl disappeared two years ago. You don't need to know her name. Her parents had money, paid a ransom, but never got their daughter back. We tracked down the kidnapper and found a receipt to Love Bot Inc. The kidnapper got double paid."

"But love bot parts only come from voluntary donors."

"Is that what you tell yourself?" she said. "The victim's parents want the rest of their daughter to bury, and they have the money to fund an investigation. How many abductions don't even get reported? How many political prisoners would voluntarily donate their bodies to something like that? Love Bot Inc had all the appropriate documentation, all forged. They still insist the body wasn't her."

She was staring at me, studying me. "Maybe," I said, "you could show me some pictures or something."

"To *help?*" She asked. "Or to give you something to fantasize about when you are with those *things?*"

"I just thought, I mean, I've been to several of those parlors."

"I bet you have."

I sank into the chair. My voice was a whisper. "You wouldn't know what it's like."

"Not to be able to get laid?"

I shot a defiant glance at her. "Exactly." Then I looked away again. "A woman like you," I said. "Strong, confident, beautiful... You don't need anyone, and when you do want someone, you can have anybody you like."

She actually blushed a little, as did I. I couldn't believe I had said that out loud. She opened her mouth, finally saying, "You'd be surprised." She cleared her throat and retrieved a file. Within were pictures of a young girl with ginger hair and a toothy smile. In one picture, under a low cut dress, a freckle pattern crept under the fabric, disappearing where a love bot's flesh would be. This girl was real, not plastic, not a machine. She had parents, friends, hopes, disappointments. Now *parts* of her were out there, serving the whims of perverts like me. I almost threw up.

"Are you okay?" Lebronski asked.

I shook my head. "What can I do to help?"

Part of me noticed her chest expanding as Lebronski took a breath, and I hated myself for it. "Continue doing what you do," she said. "The serial number on the girl's unit is *LB65244*. If you see it, call us."

"That's all? There must be something more I can do."

She shook her head. "Honestly, we've run out of leads. In the last two weeks, we've raided all the parlors we know about, but we can't be everywhere. She has to be out there."

I nodded and stood. She walked me to reception, and I looked at her one last time before I left. She gave me a nod and turned away.

I took a detour on the way home, stopped at a different truck stop on the opposite side of town. In a back room was a bot with neon blue hair and a sign that read, *SASHA*. They liked to personalize them with names sometimes.

Beside Sasha's round mouth, *cheeks* had been painted in bright pink circles. I ran my hand along her firm, tan breasts and brown areolas, not the pink of the girl I was looking for. There was a single brown freckle. A gellified layer of fatty adipose and dermis was visible where the top of the chest tissue had come loose from the chassis. I turned away, repulsed, but if I was back here too long without inserting credits, they'd kick me out. I plopped in my cards, then turned her over, let her ass face me.

"You want me, Daddy?" came a breathy voice. "You like what you see?"

Her cold ass was already warming to my touch. She had prominent dimples on the sides, and each cheek was a rounded handful. She must have been a runner. All her body hair had been removed, but the follicles rose in reaction to my fingertips.

"Oh yeah. I've been naughty, Daddy."

The whole *Daddy* thing was more distracting than arousing. I didn't want to be anyone's dad.

I spread the cheeks, seeing the two holes vibrating, forming a thin sheen of fresh lubricant. My pants were getting tight, but I wasn't here for that.

"Spank me with that cock. Show me who's boss."

I found the Serial Number in hard plastic above her left cheek. *LB65201*. It wasn't her. I let out a long breath. I felt relief, but hadn't I wanted to find the girl, show Lebronski I was worth something?

I ran my finger along the love bot's ass. I'd already spent the credits. I undid my pants. It wouldn't hurt to have a little fun.

I pressed myself against those round cheeks and found an inviting hole. I wasn't sure which one. I guess it didn't matter. I started humping. She was warm, but I was having trouble getting into it. I reached under and grabbed a firm tit.

I liked them firm like that, but I still needed something more. As long as I didn't tug too tightly on the security cable, I could pick her up. The bots weren't that heavy. I lifted her from the floor and thrust her up and down on my throbbing member. One tit bobbed free, while the other was firmly in my grasp.

"Oh, yes," came the recorded voice. "Give it to me."

That's when I again noticed the layers of loose dermis on top of the chest tissue.

"Don't stop now. Fill me up, Daddy."

I lowered her to the floor, gently turned her over, and did up my pants. I had never just watched one before. Her jerking fists vibrated mechanically against the cold floor, and her mouth and pussy hummed a constant tone. No matter how warm they made her, she was a machine with a dead woman's parts.

There was a man in a business suit waiting for the room when I left. I lowered my hat and raised my collar.

"That was quick!" the stranger said.

I wasn't accustomed to making conversation when I did things like this. "If you hurry," I said, "she still has a few minutes on her."

His eyes widened, and he rushed in.

I drove home filled with revulsion. Love bots were the only pleasure I afforded myself, but now... I didn't think they would ever be the same to me.

There was one place I could try, an out of the way place. I was already on the opposite side of town. I didn't frequent Love Shack because it was so far out, and it was a little pricier because they cleaned the bot between every customer, but I always had a special place in my heart for Betty. She had sandy blond hair, not the gaudy colors of most models, and her tits were nice C cups, just the right proportion of soft and firm. Her inner pussy lips were slightly asymmetrical, and extended just a bit beyond her outer folds when she wasn't being penetrated. A mere inch below was her puckered ass hole.

I could already feel myself getting hard.

An hour on the road, and I pulled into the drive and parked behind the Shack. I kept my hat lowered when I walked past the shelves of adult novelties and the desk clerk, who didn't look up from his magazine.

In the back room, the sign still read *BETTY*, but it wasn't *my* Betty. The bot had purple hair and large brown tits. She rested on a plump butt, a hint of cellulite between the cheeks and the back of the thighs. Some men liked a big booty like that.

I turned her over. Above the big ass was her serial number: *LB65278*.

I walked out, and the clerk looked up from his magazine. "Something wrong?" he asked.

I had never spoken to him before, always just walked past. "Where's Betty?"

"She's back there."

"No, I mean... They had a different one before."

He frowned. "Oh, that. They traded her in about two weeks ago."

"Why?"

He shrugged his shoulders. "Some sort of recall. We only keep them about a year before we trade them in anyway. They start to wear out after that."

"Where did they take her?"

The man got a sick smile on his face. "She'll be reconditioned, probably end up at a truck stop someplace, but they might offer you a deal if you want to buy her." He handed me his Love Bot rep's business card, that sick smile never leaving his face.

* * *

"You again," Lebronski said, and with a resigned tone, "Come with me."

She shut the door to her office, but I didn't sit. I gave her the address of the Love Shack.

"I know the place," she said. "We raided that one last week. Our girl wasn't there."

I tried to describe Betty, but found it impossible not to be graphic and still do her justice. "Sandy blonde hair?" I blurted out at last. "Or purple?"

She looked at her notes, then back at me. "They switched them out!" she said. "Love Bot Inc gave us the runaround, told us they didn't know where she ended up. They took her back."

I nodded and gave her the rep's business card.

"This man will be able to lead us to the body," she said. "Or to someone else who can. If he doesn't talk, he'll serve jail time." She looked at me, a brightness in her hazel eyes. "You may just bring Congressman Frehly and his family some peace at last."

"Congressman Frehly?" I said. I vaguely recalled a Congressmen Frehly who had been a vocal opponent to the president on many business-friendly policies, but I hadn't heard much about him in the last couple years.

She frowned. "I wasn't supposed to tell you that, but you've helped us so much. The kidnapping may have been politically motivated."

Lebronski was talking to me, treating me like a human being. Not just any human being, I had done something great. I straightened, and found myself a little taller than her.

She walked me to reception. "I can't thank you enough for this," she said. "You really came through."

"You'll let me know what happens?" I said.

She smiled. Actually smiled! "Of course. We'll keep you informed."

I cleared my throat. "Perhaps, when this is all settled... Maybe we could..." My throat was dry, tight... "get a coffee or something?"

She looked at me, eyes and mouth wide. The silence seemed to last forever. Finally she gave a half hearted smile, her eyes creased with concern. "I'm sorry. It's a work thing. I'm not allowed to fraternize with people I meet on a case."

I'd seen her cold to me, seen her pleased with me, and now I saw her pity me. "Sure," I said. "But I mean, after all this is over—"

"No," she said, a little of the steel returning to her voice. "It wouldn't be appropriate."

She had met me when I had my dick in one hand and a dead woman's tit in the other. I may have earned some level of respect, but she could never forget that. "Perhaps," I said, "If we'd met in some other way?"

She hesitated. "Maybe. It's possible."

I nodded and rushed out, my heart sinking into my gut. At least I had tried.

* * *

The media story blew up. Rather than be a scandal, Congressman Frehly's power was never greater. Several executives at Love Bot Inc were indicted, and many of the love bots recalled. Several truck stops voluntarily discontinued the parlors, not wanting the attention they were getting.

Over the next few months without my hobby, I managed to save up a lot of credits. I still needed to borrow money for my new toy, though. I took her out of the box and positioned the red hair. It was short, but still needed trimmed a little. This model had a bit more of a neck at the top of the plastic bean, but I still needed to cut the blue shirt in order to get it on her. I topped it off with a plastic badge from the novelty shop, and hit the button where the credit insert would have been. I'd be paying her off a while, but not spending credits each time anymore.

I looked into the painted hazel eyes and said, "I'll call you, Officer Lebronski."

"You think you can please me you worthless pervert?" came one of the prerecorded phrases. "I'd like to see you try."

I stiffened and smiled. "Oh yes."

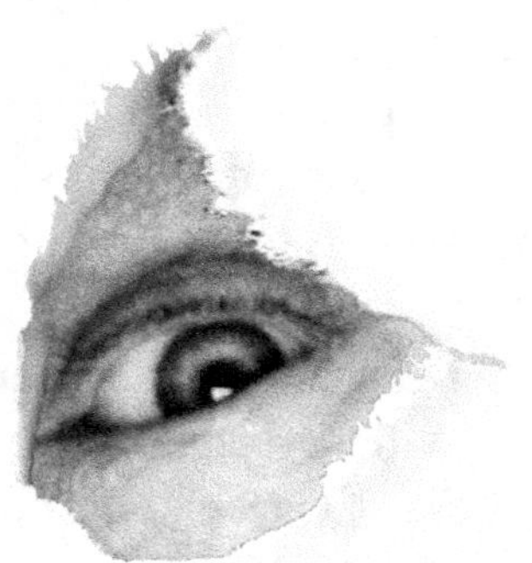

THE LIFTED VEIL

Originally published in *And the Dead Shall Sleep No More: Volume I* on October 31, 2021 by Input/Output Enterprises.

This tale took place about 250 years ago in the tiny central European village Ombra. The village sat at the foot of a big hill, and on top of that hill sat a ruined castle. Looking at the crumbling towers, you might think it abandoned, but at night, a light appeared in a single window.

Count Renaud kept to himself, but on rare occasions, he would appear in the village at twilight to buy supplies. Merchants didn't object to his money, but villagers crossed the street to avoid passing next to him. Being such a recluse, it was natural for the villagers to spread rumors about him. Every time a sheep died or a woman miscarried, they blamed it on Count Renaud.

Mae was a lovely villager of sixteen years with curly black hair and rosy cheeks. Her mother had died in childbirth. Her father adored Mae as though she were the most precious thing in the universe. With her older sister already married off, Mae took care of their little cottage. She did the laundry, cooked the meals, all the duties that a wife would usually do.

One evening, her chores all done, Mae strolled over cobblestone streets to the market in the center of town. She stopped to sniff blood red roses at a merchant's cubicle. She had a few extra coins and thought they might make the house smell nice. She didn't notice when a horse up the street got spooked and took off at a full gallop, dragging an empty cart behind him. Villagers scattered as the cart swung to the side and crashed through a vendor's booth. The world seemed to stop as the cart careened toward Mae. The wheels squeaked, and the vendor reached out to her helplessly. If the cart didn't kill her, it would tear her clothes and break her bones when it hit.

A strong hand caught the rein, and a man in a velvet coat took the impact of the cart, stopping it inches from Mae's face. You can imagine Mae's surprise when she looked up into Renaud's pale blue eyes. His wavy blond locks bounced when he turned his head, seeming to fall around his face in slow motion. White lace rose from his velvet coat and hugged his neck.

He glared as he handed the reins over to the owner of the horse. "You should be more careful!" Then he turned to Mae. "Are you hurt?"

Mae's heart raced as she tried to catch her breath. "You saved me, sir!"

"It would be a shame to see something so beautiful trampled."

She nodded. "The flowers are lovely."

"I was talking about you."

Mae's cheeks blushed as red as the roses. No one had ever talked to her like that before.

"Allow me to see you safely home."

As they walked, Mae talked to Renaud about her family and the other kids in the village. Renaud told Mae how life had changed in the village over the years, how his family had all left and how lonely life was in his castle. Other teenagers turned their heads and whispered as they passed. The attention made Mae feel special. At sixteen, she was considered almost an old maid, but none of the village boys were as fascinating as Count Renaud.

They continued talking in front of her simple cottage until Mae's father finally called to her.

Renaud took Mae's hand and kissed it, sending a tingle through her young body.

"I wish there was some way I could thank you for saving me," she said.

"There is," he said. "Allow me to walk you home again tomorrow night."

When Mae left the house to get water the next morning, she found a single red rose tucked into the doorframe.

Night after night, Renaud regaled her with amazing stories, describing life in the village as it used to be.

Her Papa and older sister warned Mae to stay away. "Nobles have no use for commoners," Papa said. "You are just a plaything to him."

Mae shook her head. "Renaud cares for me. If you could see the way he looks at me with those amazing blue eyes, you'd understand!"

Papa folded his arms. "He looks at you like I look at my lunch! Stay away!"

"What about the rumours?" her sister whispered. "That he has lived in the castle forever. That he is the reason our animals and children get sick and die."

Papa implored, "I have a sister in the city where Renaud won't find you. She can look after you."

"Why can't you be on my side?" Mae said. "Don't you think I'm good enough for a man like Renaud?"

"We are on your side!" Papa said. "We are always Team Mae."

Mae clenched her fists at her waist. "Being Team Mae means being Team Renaud too!" She slammed the door and sulked in the garden. They couldn't possibly understand how she felt. Papa had been alone ever since mother died, and Mae's sister, only seventeen, bickered with her husband like an old woman. That wasn't love.

Renaud walked her home again that evening. "What's wrong?" he asked.

"My family doesn't approve," she said. "They say that you're…" She hesitated.

"Different?" he asked.

She nodded.

"Why don't they say this to my face?"

"They're afraid you will bite off their heads."

A smile crept across Renaud's face, and he began to chuckle. "I am known for my temper. I would never hurt you, Mae, never raise my voice to you." He grabbed her hands in his. "But they are right. I am different. You've noticed how I only meet you at night, how I never share a meal with you."

Mae's heart thundered in her chest. "I don't care. I love you, Renaud."

His face lit up. "I love you too, Mae." They shared their first gentle kiss.

They continued their nightly walks until the morning Mae did not return home. In those days, when a woman moved in with a man, they were considered married, and Mae became lady of the castle. They softened the stone walls in two upper-level rooms with curtains and couches. Lanterns and a blazing fireplace bathed the rooms with warm light, and her bed was covered with quilts.

They made love for the first time early the next morning. The cock didn't crow until the first rays of sun peeked over the horizon and Mae was spent. Her fingers lightly danced across Renaud's flawless cheek. He smiled and pulled away.

"Where are you going?" she asked.

"I must return to my crypt by day. You have the run of the castle while I am asleep, but be careful. The building is old and can be treacherous."

She grabbed his arms. "Can't I come with you?"

He shook his head. "That is not possible. You must promise never to come to me while I am sleeping."

"But—"

Renaud raised his voice to Mae for the first and only time. "Promise!"

Mae nodded, and Renaud kissed her on the forehead. "The day will pass quickly. I will see you tonight."

Renaud had not been exaggerating about the state of the castle. The rough walls were bare, and furniture rotted. Only Mae's rooms were warm and furnished. After the long night, Mae slept the day away in her big, comfy bed.

Renaud pushed in a wheeled table with roasted quail and potatoes. It smelled and tasted wonderful. While Mae ate, Renaud went out for supplies. When he returned, they made love again, and again, he pulled away to sleep alone.

Night after night, the pattern repeated. Renaud brought Mae food, kissed her gently, and made love to her in the morning before retiring to sleep alone.

Mae spent her days sleeping and exploring. She mapped the castle. Down in the depths of the fortress, even at noon, no sunlight reached her. She carried a lantern down the narrow, twisting stairs. Decades of dust covered the floor, but there was a clear spot in front of an arched door where it would swivel if opened. She tugged at the door, but found it locked. She knew the sun would be setting soon and returned to her bed.

The smell of bacon and eggs woke her, and she discovered Renaud smiling down at her.

"You were sleeping so soundly," Renaud said. "I let you sleep in."

They exchanged the gentle evening kiss as they always did. She was hungry, but not for bacon. She pulled him over her.

"Your breakfast is getting cold," he said.

"But I'm all warm." For a moment Renaud seemed overcome with passion. He pulled her close, almost devouring her lips, and she didn't care if he did. She wanted to be consumed in body as she was in spirit.

But he pulled away, as he always did when night began.

"I must go into the village to gather supplies."

"Not yet."

"I must." Renaud leapt to the window and turned to her, saying "I'll be back as soon as I can," before leaping into the night.

Mae ran to the window and gazed out at the stars. Far below in one of the flickering windows, her family was sitting down to dinner.

Mae ate her bacon and picked at the cold eggs before falling asleep with her plate only half empty.

Cold hands slithered under the sheets and pulled her close. She embraced her lord without completely waking. Renaud had returned. Normally they would make love, but she was so tired.

She merely turned and latched onto him. She didn't awaken until he pulled away again.

"You just got here," she said.

"I've been lying with you for hours."

"Make love to me," she begged.

"It's too late now. Tomorrow."

"But I want you now!"

He gave her a gentle kiss. When Mae opened her eyes, she was alone.

She lay pouting for a time, but she had a plan. The next night began the same as always. Renaud prepared her meal and went out to run errands.

Mae followed the twisting path down into the depths of the castle. She found the old door and discovered, as she had hoped, that it was unlocked. She nearly gagged on the stale air within the musty room, but amid the dust was the lidless coffin she hoped to find.

Renaud returned and made love to her like he always did, but there was something even more special about it tonight. When he pulled away, she did not resist. She turned an hourglass over and waited... and waited.

The sand was not even halfway through when she descended the stairs once again.

The old door creaked open. The wax she had placed in the lock had done the trick. How surprised Renaud would be when he found her in the coffin with him the next morning. He would see that there was no harm in it, and from then on, they would be together night and day.

She brought her lantern over the coffin and saw the familiar velvet jacket, but the hands were not the smooth hands she was accustomed to. The fingers were long, and the nails like dirty razors. A bloated stomach bulged though the buttons of the faded velvet, while the rest of the body within was nearly a skeleton. A few wisps of blond hair graced a dry brown scalp. Above the moth-eaten collar, thick lips curled into a circle like a suction cup lined with concentric rows of tiny, sharp, white teeth.

This wasn't Renaud! It couldn't be!

Mae ran from the room. The echoing clang of the door made her heart jump for fear the ghoul would awaken and chase her up the steps to the warm refuge above.

She threw another log on the fire and huddled under the quilts.

It couldn't have been Renaud. She must have gotten the wrong room. When evening came, there would be some reasonable explanation, and they would both laugh.

It was no surprise when the cart rattled and Renaud's graceful steps crept into the room. She wanted to be reassured by his handsome face, but she couldn't bring herself to lift the blanket. Rough hands slid under the sheets and caressed her. It was the same familiar touch, but she had never realized how cold and dry his hands had felt before. The velvet arms of his jacket wrapped around her, and he exhaled a cold breath smelling of moldy meat. Mae clenched her eyes shut and pretended to sleep.

At last the arms retreated, but Mae remained frozen in the bed for some time before she finally turned around. A sumptuous feast sat before her, but she was not hungry.

When Renaud appeared in the window, skin stretched over his gut like a balloon ready to burst. Long fingers reached for Mae. His glistening red lips pulsated with a wet, slurping sound as he moved in for a kiss.

"Why do you pull away?" Renaud asked.

Mae's mouth quivered. She could not answer.

His dry, skeletal face cracked with sadness. "You went to the crypt, didn't you? Why? I told you not to."

She finally managed to stutter out, "What happened to you?"

He looked away from her horrified gaze. "This is the real me, Mae. What you saw before was a glamour, an illusion."

Tears dripped from Mae's eyes. "Bring it back!"

Renaud shook his head. "I'm sorry, Mae. You can't unsee what you have seen. I really do love you, Mae. I wish it didn't have to end like this."

Mae sniffled and stared into the undead face. "I love you too, Renaud. I don't want it to end."

"Can you really love this face?"Renaud moved closer. Mae leaned toward the pulsating lips and rows of sharp teeth. These were the same lips that had been kissing her all these months. Those wisps of blond hair had formed the same golden mane she had caressed when they made love. As their faces neared, she closed her eyes, wanting to let the tiny teeth caress her lips as they always had before, but at the last moment she turned away.

Renaud raised his hands into the air and howled like a dying animal. A burst of cold air blew out all the torches and candles in the bright cheery room, plunging them into darkness.

That morning, Mae appeared on her father's stoop with a suitcase. No one asked her what had happened, and she never talked about it. Any gossip about the castle's lord hushed when Mae appeared.

She sometimes gazed longingly at the castle on the hill, but the window remained dark.

Mae was still young and beautiful, but sadness now tainted her big eyes. The boys never came around, but she didn't mind. No one could ever match the illusion of love she had felt with Renaud. She dreamed about kissing Renaud as she first saw him, but when she pulled away, she faced rows of teeth and throbbing wet lips on a dry, lifeless face. She wished she would have had the strength to kiss that dead face and embrace those skeletal arms, wished he had never discovered she could see the real him.

When Papa died, Mae moved in with her sister. She doted over her nieces and nephews, and they loved her very much. Her nieces and nephews had kids of their own, and they doted over Mae. She was a graceful old woman, but no one lives forever… well almost no one.

The family cried at the funeral, but they understood the nature of life and death. A handsome man in a velvet coat watched the funeral from a distance. When the crowd dispersed, Renaud dropped a single red rose onto the grave.

"Did you know Great-aunt Mae?"

Renaud gasped when he saw the rosy cheeked girl and her curly, dark hair. "You look just like her!"

The girl chuckled. "That's silly. She was an old lady."

"We were all young once. Your aunt was a remarkable woman. What is your name, young lady?"

"Amelia."

"I am Renaud, lord of the castle."

Amelia gazed at the lifeless ruin on the hill. "No one lives in the castle."

Renaud nodded. "No one has truly lived there for many years."

"You're funny," she said.

Renaud smiled for the first time in decades. "Allow me to walk you home."

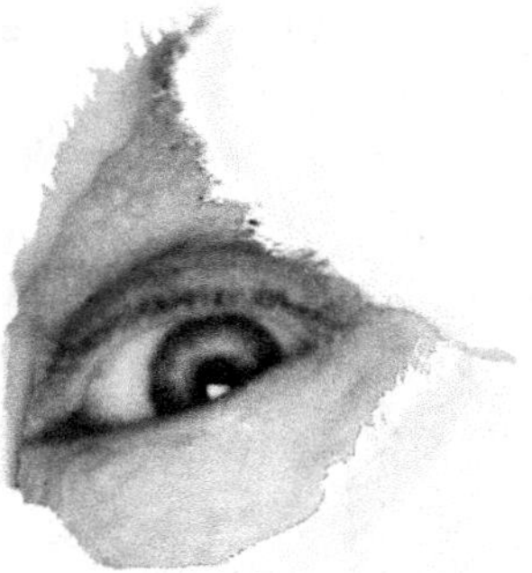

NEVER ALONE

A shortened version of this story was posted on the *Nobilis Erotica* podcast as "The Haunted Vagina" on May 18, 2024

Shadows moved across the room as headlights sped past the window. Skeletal branches caressed the closet door, but the room and the noise faded into the periphery, meaningless, as my eyes closed and my head sank deeper into the pillow at my back. The wispy voice barely registered when it spoke. All I could think of was Jacob's fingers nudging my labia aside, and his lips kissing my thighs under the sheets.

I hadn't heard the voice in over a year and hoped this must be some post-traumatic echo from my subconscious. Surely the specter had forgotten me by now.

Jacob wasn't the best looking man I had ever dated. I had a type, I suppose—tall, dark, and always ready for action. Jacob was the opposite of that, or so I thought. He was two inches shorter than me, and pale skin hugged lean muscles with a touch of softness around the love handles. When my car had a part recalled, Jacob checked my vehicle into the shop, took care of my rental while it was being fixed. He was very friendly and called with regular progress updates, but it never occurred to me he might be interested in dating until all the work was complete and he asked me out. I had been single for such a long time. If old patterns weren't working, why not try something different?

One calloused finger slid inside me, then two while his tongue lapped against my clit. It felt nice, but wasn't what I wanted. I needed him to take me now!

Jacob's question threatened to break the mood. "Elise, do you have something up there?"

I struggled to regain English language skills. "Huh?"

"Like an IUD or something? Something pinched me."

"No!" I shouted, "Nothing!" demanding, "Keep going!"

I expected this sweet guy would be less sexual than the others, which is what I was looking for at the time. I hoped perhaps I could escape my curse and my loneliness with him. I had no idea how electric his touch was or how his kisses could rip away conscious thought. All concerns of the day faded when his lips touched mine. With all that intensity, I had still managed to resist the need for months.

"What?" Jacob asked.

"I didn't say anything. Keep going."

It had been so long since I'd let a real man touch me. After almost three months of teasing, we were finally doing this. I felt like a bomb about to explode. Jacob's fingers were pruning from my wetness. I giggled, wondering how my body could make such a deluge. Where did all that fluid come from?

The grating whisper broke the mood. "Get out!"

Jacob pulled away. "Okay, I know I heard it that time!"

"It wasn't me!" I flipped Jacob over and kissed him hard. I'd waited too long for this to stop now. If I ignored it, perhaps it would go away.

My tongue probed all the way to Jacob's tonsils. He cupped one of my hanging breasts and pinched my thick, brown nipple, sending a shiver through my body. I fondled his groin. The skin was so tight over his hardened dick that I feared it might rupture. My hand glided over the pre-cum oozing from the tip.

His fingers found their way back to my loins, and I felt his cock throb in time to my moans.

He suddenly jerked my hand away from his bobbing member. "I'm sorry," he said, panting. "I don't want to come too quickly."

I smiled and kissed him again, turned on by his lack of control. "I want it quick. Quick and hard!"

I returned to my back, beckoning him on top of me. He rose, draping the sheet over us. He kissed me more gently then I wanted in that moment, but it didn't matter. All that mattered was that I was about to get fucked at last.

A cold breath billowed out from beneath the sheets and the door slammed shut, causing us both to jump.

"Just the wind," I said. If he hurried, we could be done before the ghost had time to react. Perhaps that would break the curse for good. "Stick it in!" I insisted. "It won't take me long!"

My words inspired giddy excitement. He immediately and eagerly pressed into me. My brow furrowed as I felt the pop of the glans entering me and then the stretch as his shaft pushed its way in after so many years of emptiness.

His whole body tensed as he moaned from the power of my warm, wet, clenching muscles. He seemed afraid to move.

"Yes!" I cried. "Do it!"

His eyes shot open when his deep moan transformed into a high-pitched scream. He shoved the sheet aside and grabbed the base of his shaft protruding from between my legs, trying to pull free.

I held his wrist, trying to steady him so he didn't pull too hard and hurt himself, but he didn't understand what I was doing and fought against me. "Stay calm! He won't hurt you."

"He?"

As Jacob slid further out, we could see skeletal fingers wrapped around his dick in the pale window light. "What the fuck?" Jacob tried to pry them loose, and I slammed the side of my hand against the cold digits, yelling, "Stop it, Robert! Let go!"

The hand suddenly collapsed into an ectoplasmic residue on the sheets. Jacob tumbled off the bed onto the tangled blankets. He retreated to the corner, holding himself and staring up at me with red face and watery eyes.

I clicked the bedside lamp and leaned forward on my hands. My hanging breasts cast their shadow upon the poor, confused boy. "Are you alright?"

"No! I am not alright! What the hell was that thing? It looked like a… It had to be a trick of the light."

I looked away, unable to meet his terrified gaze. "It's no trick. I'm sorry."

"You called it… Robert? It has a name?"

I began blubbering and shook my head. "I th-th-thought he was gone. I'm sorry! I h-h-hoped he was gone."

"Who?"

I brought my knees up to my chest, smooshing my breasts as I pulled inward and prepared for the inevitable rejection. "My ex-boyfriend."

Jacob cloaked himself in blankets and stood abruptly. "What?"

Impossible wetness now leaked from my eyes, much less fun than when it had dripped from my now cold groin mere minutes ago. That thought made me feel even more disappointed. "That's why I made you wait so long. You think I didn't want to make love to you before now? Hell, I would have taken you on the second date, but I didn't want to scare you off."

I heard the springs and felt the mattress sink, but when his hand touched my shoulder, I flinched.

"I don't understand," he said. "What's going on?"

I wiped my eye with the back of my hand and sucked a glob of snot back into my nose. "He's the one who dumped me! I don't understand why he is doing this."

"Back up. Your ex-boyfriend is doing this somehow, as revenge?"

I shook my head. "He killed himself the day after he broke up… in a text! But I didn't even find out he was dead for weeks. All I knew is he stopped talking to me, stopped returning my calls, stopped answering his door." The thought occurred to me that he was probably already dead when I had knocked on his door. I pushed it away.

"I tried to move on as best I could. A couple weeks later, I could tell something wasn't right. My date and I were making out at a drive-in movie when the headlights came on. I thought he had nudged the switch with his leg while he was groping me. We clicked them off, but then the radio switched stations and blared full blast. Shouts harassed us from the surrounding cars, and everyone was staring at us, throwing cups and popcorn at the car." As the memory played in my mind, the guy's face was practically blank. I'd barely known him. His black Camaro was clearer in my mind than he was. "The headlights popped back on, and the brights flipped on and off."

The muscle car had been in accessory mode so we could listen to the movie through the car's radio. I froze when the radio switched stations a second time, blaring 'Faithfully' by Journey. That song always reminded me of Rob. I remained frozen when the guy clicked the car completely off again and tried to continue his work. I no longer felt any enthusiasm as clumsy hands moved up my shirt and his tongue shoved into my mouth.

"Even with the car completely off, it happened a third time, and the crowd was becoming an angry mob. We got out of there quickly and never saw each other again. I figured it was a fluke, a problem with his car's electrical system, but the ghost chased my next boyfriend away too."

I left out the gory details of that encounter, Rob squirting green liquid into my date's bearded face in a scene right out of *The Exorcist*. I immediately scheduled an appointment, but my gynecologist said I was perfectly healthy and normal.

"I'd been cursed and didn't know why. I finally ran into Rob's sister at the corner grocery. Rob had been sick, some kind of cancer, but he never told me!" I looked up to the ceiling. "Why didn't you tell me?" I reached for the nightstand and pulled out my phone to show the photo Rob's sister had sent me. "This was in Rob's bedroom."

Jacob squinted at the photo. Mementos from the dates Rob and I had been on sat on a table: ticket stubs, printed selfies, a slip of paper from a fortune cookie, even a discarded popsicle stick. It looked like a shrine.

"She asked if I wanted any of it before she threw it all away, but all I wanted to do was forget about it. None of it was my fault. *I* didn't make him break up. Didn't make him not tell me he was sick. Didn't force him to..." I looked to the ceiling again. "You didn't even give me a chance!" I returned my gaze inward. "I jumped in bed with a man I met on an app, but it was another disaster. Rob wouldn't let me move on. I was single for almost a year before I tried to date again, but that didn't last either. After three years of celibacy, I'd hoped perhaps Rob had finally forgotten me."

Jacob's brow creased. He stared at me with wide, penetrating eyes.

"You don't believe me," I said.

He opened his mouth as if to speak, but nothing came out.

I met his eyes at last. "I really liked you. I wanted it to work out, but I understand."

"What do you mean?"

I held the pillow to my chest. "You can leave. I don't blame you at all, Jacob. They all leave me, everyone but Rob."

He pulled my head into his chest, but my body remained stiff. "I'm not going anywhere."

"You will. It's too much. You deserve a nice, normal girl."

"I don't want normal. I want you!"

I stopped crying and cocked my head up at him.

He chuckled lightly. "You know what I mean."

My muscles relaxed slightly. I looked down at his flaccid, reddened penis. "Does it hurt?"

"Only when I think about it." He pulled the sheet over us and held his naked warmth against my back. "We'll figure something out. I didn't start dating you because of sex."

I turned my head, raising a skeptical eyebrow at him.

"Well, not *just* for sex. We'll figure this thing out together. You aren't alone anymore."

I wanted to say, *I'm never alone. That's the problem,* but I kept my mouth shut. Jacob was being sweet, and I didn't want to ruin it.

Jacob's limp, bruised penis pressed against my back. The really sad thing was, I was still kind of horny, even after all of that, but the moment was over.

I lay my head back down, and he stroked my hair. Stress and exhaustion finally got the better of me. We fell asleep with the lamp on, as though the light could keep the ghost away, but Rob was always here.

***

Another sexless week passed. I didn't think it was possible to be even more frustrated. Jacob spent almost every night at my little cottage home, sleeping in the same bed, but we were afraid to cross the line, and neither of us was sure where exactly that line was. Rob seemed to be sleeping *inside* me, but awoke when things got heated.

Jacob or I would always pull away before things got too hot. We distracted ourselves with conversation and watched streaming television shows or movies when we ran out of things to talk about. Later, like an old married couple, we would sit silently working on our own interests, me reading, Jacob scrolling memes or playing games on his phone.

One night seemed innocent enough, we were just kissing on the bed when Jacob scrunched up his nose and got up to look out the window. "Someone must have hit an animal on the road."

I dramatically opened a magazine and tried to ignore him. I'd hoped the smell wasn't as strong as I feared and he wouldn't notice.

He must have seen my change of mood. "What?"

"It's me."

"It's not you," he insisted, opening the window and inhaling the cool, fresh night air. "Maybe there is a dead mouse somewhere."

I tried to focus on the magazine again while he opened the closet and examined the floor. His nostrils flared while he sniffed.

He left the closet open and neared me, still sniffing. When his head neared my crotch, I pushed him away. "I already told you. It's me, okay?"

He recoiled and held his nose.

I threw down my magazine. "I'm sleeping on the couch."

"No!" He said. "This is your house! Stay!"

"Then *you're* sleeping on the couch?"

"It's not that bad. I'll light a scented candle."

I hugged myself, knowing a candle would only add another layer of smell over the stench. "I'm disgusting."

He put his arms around me from behind. "It's not you. It's… that thing."

"Well, it's coming from *my* body, so it might as well be me!"

"I'm sure you aren't the first girl to—"

I turned my head. "To have a stinky ghost inside her vagina?"

He smirked. "Well, I don't know about that part."

I turned my body to face him. "You think this is funny?"

"No! Of course not!"

I marched out of the bedroom.

He followed. "Come on, babe."

"Don't *babe* me!"

"I'll light a candle and leave the window open. It's not that bad, really. It's already clearing out."

"But what about tomorrow night, and the night after? There will always be something."

"It's late. We're both tired. Come back to bed."

"You can't keep this nice guy act up forever."

"Let's just worry about tonight for now, okay? We can worry about forever tomorrow."

I relented, went back to the bedroom and took an over-the-counter sleeping pill. He lit a candle and turned out the light. "See, mood lighting." He crawled into bed and hugged me. "Kind of romantic."

"Seriously?"

He shrugged a shoulder. "A little."

The smell did get better, or perhaps we just got used to it.

I used to take sleeping pills occasionally to help me sleep. With all the tension and sexual frustration, I started taking a pill every night, sometimes two. It's the only way I could sleep with that man meat right next to me… right… fucking… there, brushing against me when he clung to me, bulging against me in the morning. I breathed a sigh of relief when he got up in the morning to pee. We had survived another night. But the sight of his butt as he stumbled to the bathroom was so nice.

I pretended to still be asleep when he gave me a gentle peck and headed to the auto shop.

Physical closeness led to an emotional connection at least as deep as the connections I'd felt in the past with sexual partners, perhaps even deeper, but the frustration was almost unbearable. Jacob really thought he could handle it, but he became irritable. Mundane annoyances set him off, and I started to act out, encouraging his anger as though trying to get the inevitable breakup over with, but he wouldn't leave. He was almost as persistent as the ghost.

***

Early the next week, Jacob took me to a massive stone cathedral. We walked past stained-glass windows, wooden pews, and morbid statues of martyred saints and messiahs. Father Mohr greeted us and escorted us into a rear office lined with bookshelves and file cabinets. We sat on two cushioned chairs, and the old man brought a chair out from behind the desk so he could sit across from us with no barrier between us. I felt so embarrassed listening to Jacob explain our sexual problems to the silver-haired man of God.

"I'm sure this must seem like a strange request," Jacob told him.

"You'd be surprised how many non-Catholics ask about exorcisms. The movies made us very popular, but exorcisms are a rare rite."

"Can you help us at all?"

"I could refer your case to the bishop. I know the first thing he will ask is if you've sought medical help."

I finally spoke up. "You think a medical doctor can help us with this?"

Father Mohr handed us a business card. "The church's standard procedure is to first make sure there isn't a medical cause before we intervene. This is a doctor we have used—"

"A psychiatrist?" I exclaimed. "You think we are imagining this?"

"Not at all," he said. "This is just the standard process we always follow. The doctor can refer your case to the bishop. One thing might hinder your case with the bishop however…" He paused choosing his words as he spoke to me. "An exorcism might not be necessary at all. Something much simpler may work instead."

Jacob and I both sat up attentively in our seats.

The priest continued, "The main impetus for you seeking this exorcism appears to be a desire for sex. We view sex outside of marriage as a sin. Of course, that can be remedied easily enough. Perhaps the rite of marriage would drive this spirit away. The ghost could not claim you when you belonged to another."

The blood drained from my face. Father Mohr stared, waiting for a response, and I felt Jacob's eyes on me, but I was too scared to look at the expression on his face. I didn't like the word *belonged.*

The priest's eyes softened. "The two of you appear to love each other very much."

My mouth was quiet, dry and raspy. "Jacob and I have only dated a couple months. Maybe someday, but not yet, and not because of this. Fear and desperation are not reasons to get married."

"We provide biblical-based counseling to anyone considering marriage in the Catholic church. You will have time to consider all your goals and motivations. Our objective is a happy, lifelong union in the eyes of God."

Jacob grabbed my hand gently. I'm not sure what he was thinking, but I said, "No."

"Very well," Father Mohr said. "In the meantime, I invite you to attend Sunday services with us here. A little prayer could not hurt. God always hears you." He extended his hands. "Will you pray with me now?"

I didn't want to, but Jacob grabbed one of the father's hands, and I felt pressured to grab the other while the priest prayed on our behalf, asking God to *help us with our struggles.* I guess it couldn't hurt for the priest to ask, but my stomach knotted in irritation.

My hand was cold and hard in Jacob's as we descended the cathedral steps. "This was a waste of time," I said.

"Well, we've got to try something!" he shouted

I flung his hand away, still walking. "What is that supposed to mean? You think I haven't tried hard enough to get rid of Rob?"

"I didn't say—"

"I've been to fortune tellers, séances, mediums with toy Ouija boards. At worst they are scammers, at best, all they get out of Rob are the same three words, *Mine,* or *Get out!* You really want to get married *now?* Because of *this?*"

"I don't—"

"That would be a disaster!"

"The thought of marrying me is that abhorrent to you? Why are you even with me then? Is this all there is?"

"Probably!"

He stopped.

After a few paces, I stopped too and turned to face him. "Listen, it's not that I wouldn't possibly marry you someday; this is just too early in our relationship to have that discussion."

"I know. It's just… the way you reacted… I want a future with you."

"I want one with you too, but this really might be all there is. Maybe we should end it now, save ourselves the trouble."

He grabbed my hand and pulled me along. "Nice try. I told you, I'm not going anywhere."

My heart didn't quite know what to do with such a sudden transition from anger and irritation to absolute conviction. My feet fell into pace next to him.

"It's not all for nothing. I did grab this from the baptismal." He reached into his pocket and pulled out a vial. "Holy water!"

I didn't think holy water would help anything, but Jacob's mischievous smile broke the tension, and I smiled back. He was doing his best. "I think I love you, Jacob."

"You think so?"

"I do."

***

That night we used the holy water like a douche while Jacob said a prayer he had gotten off the internet. The sudden shock of cool water made my muscles tighten, but I relaxed as the liquid gushed back out, clear and colorless. After the last drop was gone, I looked up at Jacob and smiled, feeling clean. It felt wrong to dirty myself again so soon, so we gave each other a gentle peck and held each other while we watched television. My eyes got heavy as I basked in the closeness and the feeling of cleanliness.

Jacob finally turned the television and the lamp off.

A cramp awoke me. Birds chirped outside my window in the morning sun. When I rolled over, I saw the literal writing on the wall and my heart rose into my throat. Thick clumps of rusty red spelled the word *MINE* across the wall and extended over the mirror which hung above the dresser.

Spring flowers blossomed outside, but a dark cloud hovered over this room.

Jacob still snored. When I moved my leg, I felt the moist squish between my legs. My panties were covered in matted blood. My cycle wasn't supposed to start for at least another week. During my years of celibacy, my body had run like a clock, but nothing was regular with me anymore.

I got up as slowly as I could. The creak of the bedsprings seemed so loud in the quiet room. I set a bucket in the bathtub and started the faucet before adding soap and bleach. I donned a robe and started to rinse my panties in the sink, but instead, I tossed them in the trash.

I scrubbed the letters away with a sponge, but the clotted blood was stubborn. I'd barely gotten part of the *E* rinsed away when Jacob's raspy voice asked, "What are you doing?"

I froze and clenched my eyes shut. When I opened them again, the word mocked me. Brown water squirted from the sponge as I clenched my fist. "I'm no one's property!"

"Of course not!"

"Of course?" I mocked. "The priest and you want to put a ring on me, brand me. I pounded the wall. Rob thinks he owns me!" I threw the sponge in the bucket. "What am I to you? A charity case? A challenging conquest? If you got rid of your competition, would you lose interest?"

"Where is all this coming from?" he asked in his sleepy, perplexed voice.

I let out a fake guffaw and motioned at the wall, then at him, thinking the answer obvious and angry he didn't get it. I rushed down the hall, locked myself in the bathroom and sat my dirty ass in the tub.

A knock on the door. "Babe?"

"Just go away!" I said.

"I'm not doing that."

"It's going to happen eventually anyway, you might as well go now!"

"I'm not leaving." The doorknob rattled, but the door was locked. "I'm not leaving, and I'm going to need to pee eventually. You can't stay in there forever."

"Go pee at your apartment! This is my house, and I don't want you here!" I turned on the faucet to drown him out and let the hot water rush over me full blast. Red diffused out from under me and circled the drain.

Would he finally leave? I wanted some space, but I didn't know if I really wanted him to leave.

I turned up the heat, but I was exhausting the water heater's ability to keep up. I soaped up my body and lathered shampoo into my hair. Once rinsed, I turned the doorknob and listened to the quiet house.

I don't know which possibility scared me more, if Jacob was still there or if he was gone. I tiptoed out in a towel. The bucket and sponge sat next to a pristine wall and mirror. Jacob had even dried it off after he'd cleaned it.

On the dresser sat the business card the priest had given us and a note with an appointment time.

***

Doctor Wilks looked over her narrow glasses at me. Her hair was braided tightly over her head.

After I met with her alone, she invited Jacob in to talk to her. I skimmed a three month old issue of *Psychology Today* while I sat in the waiting room.

Finally she invited me to join them. "Do you feel guilty about how your relationship with Rob ended?"

I shrugged. "He broke up with me. What do I have to feel guilty about?"

"But you believe he didn't really want to break up. You think he was trying to shelter you from his illness. How does that make you feel?"

"Are you implying this is all in my head? That I'm somehow creating these phenomena because I feel guilty?"

I looked to Jacob. "This is real! You have the bruises to prove it!"

"It was dark…"

"You have bruises!"

Dr. Wilks intruded. "The human body is capable of amazing things."

"Are you saying my body did that to him? That my pussy grabbed him and wouldn't let go?"

"What is a more likely explanation?"

"And the car at the drive-in? Did I smear my own blood on the wall? The voice…"

Jacob shrugged. "Could have been the wind, I guess."

I stared open-mouthed at Jacob. "After all we've been through and all your vaunted statements of support, now you are really denying this is real?"

"I believe that you believe—"

I stood abruptly. "I'm out!"

I was next to the truck before Jacob had even left the building. I leaned my head against the truck bed. The thought of riding home with Jacob made me sick. I whipped out my phone and opened the ride sharing app.

"Elise!" Jacob called, nearly getting hit by a car which was pulling into the parking lot.

I sped away from the truck, still staring at the app. "Go away! I'll Uber home."

"Come on. Don't walk away after all we've been through."

"Exactly!" I turned on him. "After all we've been through! And you've just been humoring me this whole time!"

"That's not true!"

"Then when did you stop believing me?"

"Never! But Dr. Wilks made some convincing arguments— it just made me wonder is all. I didn't stop believing you. I just started asking questions. Have you never doubted the ghost, or maybe parts of it?"

I turned away again. Perhaps I had. Perhaps that's why I was really so angry. If I had trouble believing it, how could I expect anyone else to? What if some parts were real and others my imagination? Could I have written on the walls in my sleep? Could the headlights and radio at the drive-in have just been an electrical short, and I gave it meaning it didn't really have? How could I sort out the difference? How could I trust anything if I couldn't trust myself?

"I've been doing some reading," Jacob said.

"That must have been a new experience for you."

He paused with an exasperated breath. "Some folks say that ghosts aren't the same as living people, that they are just echoes of their strongest emotions."

"What do you mean?"

"Maybe this guy, your ex, had his reasons for doing what he did—stupid reasons. But the thing that came back when he died… It's not him, or… at least not all of him. He's not all there—just pieces, urges."

I paused, pondering his words.

"So, we've been trying to figure out what it's thinking, what's motivating it. Maybe there is no reasoning with this thing."

I'd spent years asking the ghost why it was torturing me, what it wanted from me. Perhaps it didn't know. I'd let the ghost taint my memory of the living Rob, the man I had loved, and on some level that I'd been denying, still loved. My own higher brain functions started alleviating *my* fear and fury, and I wondered, "Perhaps Rob has no higher brain functions anymore."

"Perhaps not. Just raw emotion. Can I take you home now, please?"

I cancelled the ride on my app. "Okay."

After Jacob had fallen asleep that night, I opened the pic of Rob's shrine. I zoomed in on two slips of paper below the printed selfies, fortunes from the Chinese restaurant on our first date. I thought we'd tossed them with our used napkins.

Rob had insisted on saying, *in bed,* after the fortunes. His read, *You've come so far...* Rob added, "*in bed,*" and laughed and laughed. I said, "It's not that funny," which made him laugh harder until I finally cracked up too. Mine read, *Your ability to juggle many things will get you far.* Rob said, "Oh, please don't do that in bed!" I pointed out that neither of them were really fortunes.

On the other side of the shrine were two ticket stubs to a Journey tribute band called Travelled. Rob had gotten the tickets because I wanted to go. I had to nudge him to keep him from smacking his chewing gum during the performance. He was more worried about traffic after the show than the show itself, but his eyes sparkled when he watched me, and I loved how he held me from behind while they played 'Faithfully.'

We'd made love for the first time after that show. Rob was so attentive, covered my entire body with tender kisses. He insisted on leaving the lights on. I felt self-conscious the first time he'd gone down on me. No one had ever paid that much attention to my nether regions. He seemed fascinated, staring at my labia as he spread them apart, eyes and mouth wide with fascination, like a kid with a new toy, or a patron gazing at a work of art. "It's beautiful," he whispered. I briefly wondered if he'd never seen one before, but he seemed to know his way around.

I never felt self-conscious with him again. I had already come when he mounted me and gently rocked back and forth. He stared into my eyes with this goofy but charming grin on his face.

His mouth opened slightly, and his brow furrowed, but he never turned his eyes away from mine, even when he was coming.

I'd never cried over Rob until that night. When he dumped me, I was too angry to cry, and then, when I found out he'd killed himself, I didn't know how to feel. I was just numb. When his ghost chased away all my attempts at moving on, anger was all I had.

***

The pepper-bearded man wafted pungent incense around the musty back room. My neck was tense as I swiveled my head on the pillow, watching him. Candles encircled us, casting faint golden shimmers over cinderblock walls. Behind my head, a tapestry hung on the wall with a design cobbled together from at least three different religions, probably more. I felt vulnerable with no bra and this thin, simple garment pulled up over my spread legs. Jacob was crouching next to the mats and pillows holding my hand like we were in some sort of demented birthing scene.

The old man's beads dangled over me, and he squeezed my breast hard.

I could feel Jacob's hand tighten. "The ghost isn't in her breasts."

Swarmi Jo didn't let go, but tilted his gaze to Jacob. His breath smelled like sour milk. "I must treat the whole body. For this to work, I must coax the spirit out before I can purge it. You both want this to work, don't you?"

Jacob looked away in silence.

"Of course, Swarmi Jo," I said. "We're desperate. We'll take any chance. Proceed."

Candlelight glinted in Swarmi Jo's gray eyes, and his mouth crooked in a smile. "Swami," he corrected me.

"Of course, Swami Jo."

He nodded, slid a rough hand beneath the threadbare garment and manipulated my breast. Perhaps I should have felt violated, but the motion was so mechanical, and I'd experienced so much over the last few years that this just felt like a creepy doctor visit. Jacob's presence helped me feel safe and protected. Swarmi

Jo's hand slid down between my legs and rubbed up and down my slit, but my vagina clenched shut like dry sandpaper.

"You must relax for this to work."

I closed my eyes and willed my muscles to loosen. The incense didn't cover the smell of Swarmi Jo's B.O. He lifted the garment to my neck and kissed my nipple, covering it with his sour saliva.

"Really?" Jacob said.

"It's necessary," said Swarmi Jo as he proceeded. His robes bulged awkwardly at the crotch, and I could tell he wasn't wearing any underwear. He finally lowered his head between my legs, and his fingers spread my labia apart. My muscles spasmed, and air hissed out. A confused look graced his wizened brow and he leaned in. "What?"

My labia twitched in time to the elongated vowels. "Get… out!"

Swarmi Jo backed away, startled. "I can't help you!"

Jacob and I shouted in unison. "You have to!"

"You insisted you could!" I said. "We put up with all your crap!"

"And paid you a shitload of money!" Jacob added.

"Full refund." His back was to us, and he exited the room. Through the beaded curtain, shelves of polished gemstones and scented oils sparkled in golden light from the display windows.

I shot to my feet. "All Rob did was speak one time, and that scared you off? You said you were an expert!"

With a wave of his hand and a shake of his head, the front door dinged and fell shut. We stood alone in his completely abandoned shop.

Jacob and I looked at each other, and my shoulders sank. Jacob went behind the counter, and the cash register dinged. "He said *full refund!*"

I gave Jacob a brief smile and put on my pants.

***

But that night, I thought the damn had finally burst in a good way. Instead of leaving, Jacob came to me while I slept, stroked me. I smiled in the dark and pinched my own nipple, releasing quiet moans. My movement became more exaggerated as the sheets twisted around my legs and my hips jerked back and forth. It had been so, so long. I needed this. My moans filled the house. "Oh, Jacob!"

The lamp clicked on, and I opened my eyes to see Jacob fully clothed in the doorway with his hand on the light switch. "I was alone?"

He narrowed his eyes. "You weren't really alone, were you? I've stayed with you through all this, slept beside you, denied myself all pleasure, then I find you fucking that thing!"

"I was not fucking anything!"

"What would you call it? Maybe you actually like this thing. Maybe you love it. Maybe you never wanted me at all."

"Of course I want you! Why are you so mad now? It grabbed you, hurt you, but *this* is what pisses you off? The idea that I might actually enjoy something."

"Yes, damn it! You think I'm enjoying any of this? And now I find out you like getting raped by that ghost?"

Fury bubbled up within me. "Never ever say that word to me! I've borne this curse way longer than you. You have no right to judge me!"

He slammed the bedroom door. I stared at the closed doorway for a time, waiting for him to come back. But the truck ignition turned over and tires spit gravel as he left. I collapsed in a heap onto the bed. Didn't Jacob understand it was him I had been thinking of? But it hadn't been Jacob in reality. Perhaps Jacob was right.

I marched to the kitchen and stuck my hand into a cabinet, reaching all the way to the back. Cans and boxes fell out, forgotten and unimportant in my quest for any small relief. The vodka burned as I guzzled straight from the bottle and leaned against the counter.

For a few days I had thought true happiness was within my grasp. I'd thought I finally found someone who would fight for me no matter what, and that, even without sex, perhaps I could still get my happily ever after.

I looked down at my abdomen. "Damn you!" I screamed, running to the bathroom with the vodka still in my hand. I yelled at my own face in the mirror as though that were the ghost. "Do you want me to be alone forever?"

I turned on the curling iron and took another long drink. I stared at the metal until I could smell the heat. "Is this what you want? For me to never feel sexual pleasure again?"

I took another long gulp. My hand shook as I put one leg on the toilet and held the iron close. Thunder shook the house, and the power went out. I could see my breath condensing in the sudden chill. I tossed the cold iron down. "Then what do you want from me?"

The lights flickered back on, and words were written through frost on the mirror. *I love you.*

I leaned on the counter, cackling. "You call this love?"

The phone buzzed with a text from Jacob. *I'm sorry. This hasn't been easy for me, but I shouldn't have taken it out on you. You are right. I don't understand. But I love you. I just need a little time. I'll be back.*

"He's coming back…" I said it joyously, but tossed the phone down and wiped the snot from my nose. "He deserves better."

My hand found the sleeping pills. I took half the bottle and washed it down with more vodka. The power went out again. "Nice try," I said, chuckling. "I'm in control now." The rest of the pills went down. My abdomen gurgled, and I responded. "Why not? You did it?" The words *I Love you* were fading with the cold on the mirror. "I loved you too, once. Is this what it felt like for you when you ended it?"

The power came back on, and 'Stayin' Alive' by the Bee Gees blared on the wireless speaker. I cackled with glee as I strutted to the beat, rolling my hands and pointing like a clumsy John Travolta. "If so, this isn't so bad!"

The phone rang, but no one was there. I spoke into the receiver anyway. "Nobody home! Just my haunted pussy!" I tossed the phone away and laughed while I danced, even though it really wasn't that funny. I paused, realizing it wasn't actually funny at all, and that made me laugh even harder.

I finally fell onto the bed. The television came on, switching channels, volume raising and lowering as my eyes became heavy. With a quiet chuckle, I said, "Aw, you're playing me a lullaby." My eyes remained closed longer each time I blinked, and I realized each time I closed them, I might never open them again. "Is this what you wanted, Rob? For us to be together?"

The lamp brightened, and my arm was too heavy to shield my eyes from the intensity. It became too bright for the bulb, and the glass popped.

My eyes opened just long enough for a quiet chuckle before I closed them again. Only the blaring television gave any illumination, but even that was forgotten. Thoughts drifted to Jacob. Would he blame himself? It wasn't the sweet boy's fault. I needed to get up, to write a note, explain, but my body wouldn't move. "No," I squeaked out. I'm not sure if the next part was out loud or in my head. "Not yet."

I was only vaguely aware of an arm around me, lifting me. "Rob?" If I said it audibly it was unintelligible. The bed smelled like vinyl, and the television sounded like a truck motor.

My eyes drifted slowly open, but shut again to block out the fluorescent lights. Someone was in the room. I felt them staring at me, but kept my eyes shut.

Jacob's voice—"Are you awake?"

After a long pause, he pushed away the white sheet that had been covering me and lifted the hospital gown so he could stare directly between my legs. "Look," he said. "We both love Elise, but you are hurting her! You have to know you are tearing her apart! I'm not going anywhere, and neither are you. We're going to have to learn to live with each other." A nurse came in and Jacob quickly dropped the sheet. I smiled, both at his embarrassment and his sweetness.

"I see our patient is awake," the nurse said.

Jacob saw me watching him, and his face flushed while the nurse took my vitals and asked me questions.

When she finally left, Jacob and I spoke simultaneously, "I'm sorry."

My fingers felt like pins and needles when he grabbed my hand. My skin had a grayish tint which disturbed me. I was afraid to ask how close to death I had actually come.

"I should never have left."

I shook my head. "I did something stupid. That wasn't because of anything you did. You had every right to be upset. It's been difficult for both of us. I love you! Thank you for coming back."

"I wasn't going to."

My eyes shot up.

"I mean not yet. I would have come back, just not that night, but my phone kept buzzing. No one was on the other end of the line. Then the truck died. I coasted to the side of the road. It started right back up again, and the radio played 'Help' by the Beatles. I turned down the volume, went forward a few feet, but the truck died again. I cranked the key and started her up again. Now the radio was playing 'I need a hero' by Bonnie Tyler. Again it died as soon as I inched forward. I was thinking about what could cause the problem when I started it again. The radio was now playing 'Come to My Window' by Melissa Etheridge. The headlights flashed on and off. My phone kept buzzing. I turned the steering wheel and did a U-turn, going back the way I'd come, and the truck ran fine. I couldn't figure out why Rob would want me to go back when he had been trying so hard to get rid of me this whole time."

"You called him by name! Not *the ghost,* or *that thing.*"

"When I found you, I understood. He had called me for help." A tear dripped from his eye. "He saved your life."

I took his hand in both of mine, kissed it, and held it to my heart, which was still beating because of my two boys. "You both saved me."

***

I unbuttoned my skirt and let it fall to the floor. "Are you sure about this?" I asked.

"We'll go slowly. Things might be different now. I think we've all come to an understanding." Jacob looked down at my panties. "Haven't we, Rob?" Jacob paused, but there was no response.

I pulled Jacob's chin to my face. "What if I don't want to go slow?"

He smiled and kissed me, much too gently. I shoved my tongue into his mouth and sucked on his lips. We felt our way onto the mattress, continuing to kiss. I could no longer tell where my lips ended and his began. All I knew was the desperate need for contact. No amount of touch was enough. I wanted him all.

His fingers probed up my thigh and under my soaked panties. Only then did I realize how wet I had become. When did that happen?

He began to lower my panties, but I grabbed his jeans instead and yanked them down. I couldn't get them off fast enough. His penis throbbed in my mouth, and I could taste his salty eagerness.

I slid off my panties and groaned as I mounted him.

He clenched his eyes shut, and his mouth narrowed into a thin line. I became worried. "Are you okay?"

"I don't want to finish too quickly."

I laughed. "We've both waited a long time for this."

"Exactly! I don't want to disappoint you."

"You won't disappoint me as long as you relax and enjoy it. I want to feel you get off inside me."

He flipped me over and took control, easing into me.

"Harder!" I demanded.

He shook his head, his face all red as he fought the urge to come. "I can't!" Suddenly, his face relaxed and his eyes grew wide.

"What's wrong?"

"I don't feel anything."

For a moment I was offended. He pulled out and checked himself. "Everything seems to be working correctly."

I gritted my teeth in frustration. "Take me!" I demanded.

He shoved into me, rougher this time, but still slow and steady.

"Faster!" I demanded. "Harder!"

He followed commands, building in speed and power. I reached behind him and felt his ass clenching and releasing as he pounded into me. I could no longer tell when he was in or out. It all blurred together into one massively pleasurable sensation tingling from my groin all through my body in waves as he thrust, fast, hard, steady.

I forgot where I was and what my name was and I didn't care. My body clenched and tightened—so soon? Not quite. I relaxed again. Then suddenly, without warning, my body became rigid and silent. I slammed my fist on the mattress under me. "I… told…you…wouldn't…take…" I let out a guttural groan, loud at first but then suddenly soft. I lay there catching my breath as he continued to thrust.

"Oh!" He said. "I can feel again, but…"

"What?"

"It's kind of… loose."

"I already came." It was my turn to worry. My formerly tight pussy had collapsed into exhausted jelly. I'd come so hard for the first time in so many years that it needed time to recover. It had never occurred to me that I might disappoint Jacob. "I'm sorry."

"No!" he said, continuing to push into me. "You had fun, right? That's what matters to me. You want me to stop?"

"No! –Oh?" I could feel something moving above his penis. It took a moment to understand what it was. The hood around my clit was twitching, slipping up and down on its own. There was no shortage of lubricant down there, that's for sure. the sensation was almost too intense to withstand, but I didn't want it to stop.

He almost laughed. "You're getting tight again!"

"Oh…" My voice dropped an octave. "God." Rob stimulated my clit while Jacob stretched my pussy. "Yes!" I thought about how anticlimactic this might appear from the outside. No one could see Rob's manipulations. We weren't filming a porno for other people's pleasure. We were the only three entities in the universe who mattered.

Jacob grunted and groaned on top of me like an animal. I moaned, and his penis throbbed in response to my voice. I stared into his growling face. It looked like he was concentrating, resisting.

"Come in me!" I demanded.

He yelled as he pulsed inside. The sudden, spurting warmth triggered me again, and I clenched my eyes shut in silence before shouting, "Holy fuck!"

He slowed his thrusts as I melted into goo underneath him and he finally collapsed. I stroked his sweaty back and listened to him pant.

He began to chuckle. I didn't know why, but I laughed too, saying, "That was amazing!"

He agreed. "Well worth the wait!" He rolled off and caressed my stomach. He leaned over my vagina and whispered, "Thank you, Rob."

A wide grin grew on my face. My two boys were getting along, and I felt like the luckiest girl in the world.

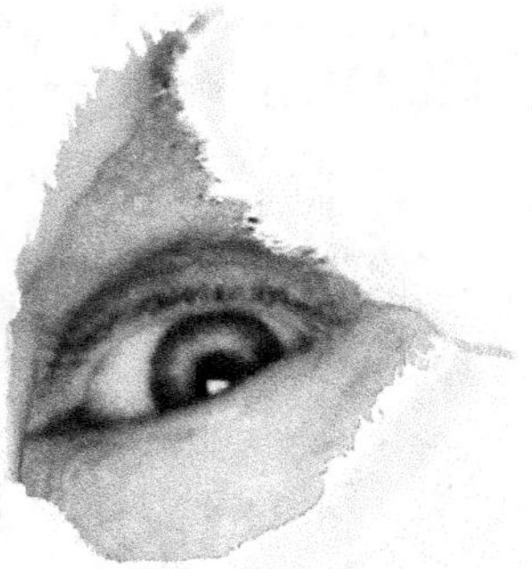

THE DEVIL IN HIS PANTS

Originally published in *Devilish Deals* from Thurston Howl Publications November 23, 2022

The pressure in Jake's jeans hurt. He pulled his shirt down over his pants and wiped his sweaty palms on the cotton.

Megan straightened up from the counter and pulled the neck of her shirt up. Had he been staring? Her bra pushed her breasts up and together under her nametag.

"Can I help you?" she asked.

He looked up into her blue eyes. Were those long lashes natural, he wondered, or painted on somehow? His heart pounded against his chest.

Jake's high, raspy voice cracked as he spoke. He hated the sound of it. "Have you thought any more about going out tonight?"

Megan let her mouth hang open. "I can't tonight. There are people in line behind you. Do you need to take out some money?"

"No." He looked behind him at the line of people. One woman scowled, complaining about the line to a friend on her cell phone. "Wait," Jake said to Megan. "I'll take out fifty."

Her long fingers blurred across the keypad. She had his account number practically memorized.

"What about tomorrow?" Jake asked.

"This isn't a good time. Why didn't you call me?"

"The number you gave me doesn't work."

Megan wrote a phone number on his receipt. "I changed numbers," she said quietly. "Jake, I'm sure you're an alright guy, but you need to work on your approach. Call when I'm not working." She looked behind him and raised her voice. "Next."

He turned to leave. The people in line behind him breathed a collective sigh of relief.

Jake normally wasn't able to approach girls so aggressively. He and Megan had gone to school together. The familiarity made talking to her easier.

The pressure in his crotch had subsided, but when he looked down, he found the bulge remained. Jake stopped in the restroom. Adjusting his member up made it less visible through his pants, but on thinking of Megan, the pain returned. He locked the stall door. In mere seconds, Jake wiped his shame off the plastic seat with some toilet paper and flushed it away.

Jake washed his hands and left with his pants loose and relaxed.

He gave one last look over his shoulder at Megan as he walked out the glass doors. Was this her real number, he wondered, or just a ruse to get rid of him?

A young girl in line at the post office wore short-shorts. Denim crept up her butt cleavage and left half moons of brown muscle hanging over the back of her thighs.

His pants tightened again, and Jake shouted down at his crotch. "Oh, come on!"

The girl gave him a confused, frightened look, and Jake turned toward the post office boxes.

Did other men have this problem? Women thought he was creepy, and premature erections weren't a turn on. If he could just get laid once, the problem might go away, but he was destined to die alone.

Jake's heart leapt with hope at the small brown package inside his mailbox. He'd been awaiting the final ingredient for over a month.

* * *

Jake threw the gnarled mandrake root into the food processor. It ground and buzzed violently. He feared the blades would break against the tough fiber, but the grinding subsided into an even hum, and he added the other ingredients.

Jake spread the resulting paste out on a cookie sheet. The mixture took forever to dry in the oven. Ready-made powder hadn't done anything. Making it all himself had to work.

A bar separated the living room from the kitchenette. The room was dark except for the circle of candles on the hardwood floor. Mounds of dirty laundry seemed to undulate in the flickering, orange light.

What would his parents say if they saw him burning the homemade mélange in the center of the circle? They were good, God-fearing folk. He had done as they would do, prayed for help. None came.

This was just another kind of prayer. Within the flames was a slip of paper with the name of a different god.

Flame gave way to smoke and the smell of rotten eggs. His groin ached with anticipation.

He collapsed on his knees and waited. The stinky cloud obscured the candlelit room in a brown film.

He continued to sit.

After twenty minutes, Jake finally blew out the candles. He had spent all his money on a fool's hope.

A faint crunching froze Jake before a darkened candle. It sounded like rodents crawling through the walls. Something wormlike poked up through the blackened powder. The slender digits were tipped with polished fingernails. Hands pushed floor and ash aside.

A lithe body wound its way up through the hardwood. The mystery woman waved back and forth like a dancing cobra, or a belly dancer with no spine. Though her body swayed, her round breasts remained trained on Jake. The fullness of her face gave it a quality of youthful innocence. This quality was ruined when she opened her eyes. Where her eyeballs should be, tufts of curly hair sprouted from the sockets. Her nipples were eyes staring Jake in the face.

"Well?" The demoness said.

Jake stood speechless. Mouths in her palms breathed deeply of his nervous sweat.

"Trouble with the ladies?" she said.

"Yes," Jake said. "Women don't like me. I want women to like me."

One breast remained focused on his face. The other looked down at his crotch. "A strapping boy like you?"

Jake thought he should be repulsed by the sight of her, but the dancing hips, the waving arms and the observing breasts aroused him.

She smiled, revealing shark-like teeth. "You like?"

Did she mean to have sex with him? He couldn't see any legs below her hips. If she had any, they were still below the floor, but certainly not in the apartment below. He wondered how a demon like that made love.

Her eye sockets stared blindly at the wall behind him. "What would you give for this?" she asked. "To have any woman you want?"

He had known this was coming. "I will give you my soul."

"But we already have that," she said.

"What do you mean?" Had the act of summoning her sealed his doom, or had they owned him from the start? Perhaps the fate of men's souls was preordained.

"What will you give?" she asked again.

"What do you want?" Jake asked.

Her body waved back and forth while her breasts gazed into him in silence.

"I'll give you anything!"

She smiled and grabbed his shoulder. The mouth in her hand bit into his flesh.

She pressed her other hand violently against his crotch. His lungs seized. Jake instantly had something like a dry orgasm and fell to the floor.

* * *

The whine of the smoke detector woke Jake. His shoulder was intact, not even sore. He touched his crotch and found it soft and healthy. He turned off the alarm, opened a window and got a fan to blow the fetid air out.

A tiny pile of smoldering ash remained in the center of the circle, but the floor was solid. Had it all been in his mind?

All he could think about was Megan.

He didn't even put on a jacket before running out of the apartment and into the night. A couple made out on a park bench. The girl pushed her date away and stared at Jake as he passed.

He must have looked a sight. He sniffed his t-shirt and found he was still covered in that sulfurous smell.

He buzzed the outer door of Megan's building, a large house that had been partitioned into apartments. She wasn't home, of course. It was Friday night, and someone like her obviously had plans.

He sat on her front stoop and exhaled. Jake let his head rest on his arm. He hadn't realized how exhausted he had been.

"It's someone I know from school."

Jake awoke with hard cement jabbing into his back. Megan stood over him with a well-dressed man at her side. What a fool Jake had been! Sleeping on her stoop like a bum, smelling of sweat and sulfur! And there she was, fresh from her date, more beautiful than he had ever seen her. The man on her arm could have been a model.

"You want me to talk to him?" her date said.

"Go home," Megan said. "I'll handle him."

"You want me to leave you with him out here?"

"I've got it," she insisted. "Call me tomorrow."

"I don't like it," he protested once more. "This is weird!"

"Just go!"

The man scowled at Jake and walked slowly away. The man had, no doubt, imagined the date ending very differently.

Megan's eyes softened.

"I was out for a jog," Jake said. "I just sat down for a minute. I didn't realize where I was. I'm leaving."

"No!" She said. "You look exhausted. Why don't you come up for a drink? It will get your energy back up."

Jake couldn't believe his ears.

She led him by the hand into the interior hallway. Once through her apartment door, she tossed down her purse. Without a word, she pressed against him. Her soft lips gnawed on his.

"What's wrong?" She asked. "Isn't this what you wanted?"

He stared into her porcelain face. "Yes."

Her hands roved roughly, almost painfully up and down his back.

She backed away and released the top button on her blouse. Her shirt fell to the floor. Then her bra slipped off, and her voluptuous breasts fell free. Without the bra's support, her breasts sagged under gravity's pull.

She ripped open his shirt and sucked on his nipple. "Ouch!" Jake said.

She returned to his lips. Soft breasts squished against his bare chest. Jake was living his fantasy, but something was missing.

Her tongue made its way down his neck. She was trying to be erotic, licking his stomach, but there was no mystery in the hurried way she found his pants and undid the zipper.

She took his limp member in her mouth and sucked with a throbbing, pulsating pressure.

"Don't you like it?" she asked.

"This has never happened to me before." He didn't want to admit the full truth of that statement. Jake had never been naked with a woman. His nerves must have affected him. Why did his penis choose now to be unresponsive when he normally couldn't turn it off?

She pushed him onto the couch. "Sitting is better for the circulation."

She might as well have been sucking on his finger.

"Listen," Jake said. "You can stop."

She sucked with more vigor, humming with a fake enthusiasm Jake recognized from a hundred pornos.

"You can stop," he said again.

At last he stood, pushing her away. She grabbed his member violently and pulled him painfully toward her. He yanked her hand away and pulled up his pants.

"Maybe we could just watch some TV," he said.

"I can do better," she said, eyes pleading.

"I'd better go," Jake said. "I'm sorry. It's my fault. I'll call you tomorrow."

"You better."

It was too much for Jake, this happening all at once. He needed to take things slower. "We can have a proper date tomorrow," he said.

She gave him a goodbye kiss that could melt paint off the wall, but Jake felt nothing. He ran down the hall and out the main door.

* * *

The next morning Jake awoke relaxed and alert. He had slept late. He kicked off the sheet and looked down. His penis, normally the thing that woke him in the morning, remained limp and lifeless.

He shook it. "Wake up, little guy. It's alright. We're alone."

He got out his porno magazines and covered himself with lotion, a Saturday morning tradition. Back and forth he stroked the lifeless, hanging flesh.

"What's wrong with you?"

He dressed and took the trash out. The neighbor girl from downstairs sat on the outside step with her nose buried in a book. Her short hair was red today. It was different every time Jake saw her. Her pear shaped body was squeezed into torn jeans. A black sports bra showed through her white tank top.

"Hey, Jake." she said.

"Hey," he said. "Reading anything good?"

"No. I just had to get out of the apartment. Cable's out. Roomate's asleep. Bored." She looked Jake up and down. "There's something different about you, Jake."

He recognized the look. Perhaps this was what he needed, a test drive with someone who wasn't as important to him as Megan. "You want to watch some television at my place?" he asked.

"Sure."

Even with the windows open, the apartment still stank of rank magic. The piles of dirty laundry and molding dishes probably didn't help.

She circled the apartment. "Wow, Jake. You need a maid."

"Are you volunteering?" He couldn't believe his newfound bravado.

"Yeah, right. I don't even clean our apartment."

She stopped in front of the bedroom and smiled. The magazines were still spread over the bed next to the lotion.

"You weren't bored, were you, Jake?"

"No. I was just—"

"I know what you were doing, Jake, but I'm here now." She pressed her young body against him, but he felt nothing. "What's the matter, Jake? You prefer your magazines?"

At last, he couldn't take it anymore. He pushed her away and out of the apartment.

She pounded at the door. "You can't get away with this, Jake! Fucking perv."

* * *

That night, Jake and Megan tried again to make love. Even on top of her, their naked bodies intertwined, his body wouldn't respond.

There could be no doubt. The ritual had done something to him. He could get any woman he wanted, but couldn't act on it.

He needed to summon up the demoness again, get the spell removed. He had spent more than he could afford gathering the ingredients the first time.

Megan lay beside him in the bed. Her fingers danced lightly on his bare chest. "Don't worry," she said. "This happens to guys. At least, I've heard that it does. It'll pass."

She looked at him as though she really cared.

"I might be able to fix it," Jake said, "but I need money."

She grinned. "I can get money."

She snuggled into his arms. Would she still care if the spell were reversed? A moment like this was worth impotence, but the magic was frustrating Megan, and it frustrated Jake to watch her suffer. She needed a whole man. Jake prayed that man would be him.

* * *

Jake placed the flaming mojo in the center of the candles. The smell, after a week of cleanliness, made him want to vomit. Megan had taken a day off work to clean his apartment for him, which seemed out of character. Jake wondered how much of the Megan he had spent time with was really her, and how much was the magic.

He called the demon woman by name and waited.

After twenty minutes he called to her again. With tears in his eyes, he begged to have her gift removed.

His groin twitched, and his tears stopped. His member wiggled back and forth, struggling to be free.

Jake giggled and unzipped his pants.

He gasped. There on a bed of curly hair, instead of the familiar sight, rose the miniaturized, swiveling waist of the writhing demon woman. There was no distinction where his skin ended and hers began. Her shark-like mouth laughed silently as her breasts witnessed the horror on Jake's face.

Jake's breath came in quick, shallow gulps. Even with his eyes clenched, he could feel her undulating back and forth. He hated the demon, but he hated himself more. He had given himself to her.

His pain was even worse now that he knew what it was like to have someone care.

He rifled through the kitchen drawers. Ever since the apartment had been cleaned, he couldn't find anything. At last he found the meat cleaver. He raised it high into the air.

She actually looked frightened.

How much of himself was left? If he brought the blade down, he wouldn't be a man anymore.

He heard a door outside the apartment and thought of the neighbor girl—so young, so vivacious. Horror and self-hatred were replaced by animalistic need. The demon licked her lips. A week of suppressed urges hit Jake all at once.

* * *

Jake never saw Megan again. He had to leave town to keep himself away. If he had tried to say goodbye, he wouldn't have been able to stop himself from taking her. If he had tried to warn her, she wouldn't have been able to stay away from him.

None of them could ever stay away.

He couldn't bear the thought of seeing Megan killed like all the others, consumed by the devil in his pants.

BACK TO NORMAL

An adaptation of this story originally appeared
in the *Dread Machine* October 1, 2021

The doorbell chimed, and I clenched my eyes shut, burying my head. The blanket felt soft and warm like always, and the sheets smelled of fabric softener, like they always did. It was as though nothing had happened. The doorbell rang again, and I half expected the lump at my side to yell at me for being too slow to answer, but the mounded blanket remained motionless.

The doorbell rang once more. I stepped into my slippers and slipped a robe over my nightgown. Sunlight beamed into the living room through the bay window, and I could see old Mr. Peterman standing on my porch in his shorts and flip-flops. He looked around the suburban street, and then, instead of ringing again, he knocked this time, apparently losing patience.

Mr. Peterman was a retired gentleman—always home, always alert. He must have heard Ethan and I fighting last night, must know something had happened.

Perhaps he just wanted to make sure I was alright.

I cautiously cracked the front door open.

Mr. Peterman studied my face, then smiled broadly and lifted a handful of envelopes and paper. "They delivered your mail to my box again. There are some bills in there, thought I better hand-deliver them."

I stared at him for a time. How could he not feel the emptiness in the room, or the guilt in my gut?

His smile wavered. "Joanie? Everything alright?"

I forced a smile. "Of course. Thank you. That was very kind of you."

Peterman shrugged. "No trouble at all. I saw the car in the driveway—"

Here it came. He saw that Ethan hadn't left for work and knew something was wrong.

But instead of asking about my husband, Mr. Peterman went on and on about the shrubs that bordered our yards and a new kind of insect killer. Finally, I excused myself from the conversation, thanked him again, and shut the door tightly with a perverse smile. I had done it! I had gotten away with murder!

Of course no one would suspect me! Not quiet little Joanie.

Joanne, I corrected myself. People only called me *Joanie* because that is what Ethan called me, at least when he wasn't calling me *idiot.* I wasn't Joanie anymore.

My heart skipped when the phone rang. It rang and rang. *Joanie!* I expected to hear, *Answer the damn phone,* but it stopped ringing, and I fell to the floor laughing. No one had said anything. No one complained.

No one cared.

I stopped laughing and listened. The house creaked just a bit when the wind blew. It was so quiet. I didn't have to make Ethan's breakfast or pack his lunch, didn't fear what he might do if I made the wrong sandwich or packed the wrong snack.

I jumped when the phone rang again, reached for it, but stopped myself. When the ringing finally ceased, I checked the caller I.D. It was the warehouse, probably calling to see why Ethan hadn't come to work. I couldn't keep this quiet forever.

In the bedroom, the lump remained as I had left it. *You idiot!* I heard his voice. *You'll never get away with this. You're too stupid.*

Ethan would have known what to do. I was always so unsure, but Ethan was decisive. He grabbed what he wanted. He didn't always choose the right thing or the smart thing, but he always knew what to do, and that's how it was done.

He used to say he could kill me if he wanted, make it look like a suicide. *And everyone will believe it, 'cause no one would believe someone as stupid and ugly as you would want to live.*

"You didn't think I was stupid or ugly when you married me!" I said to the lump.

I *didn't know you were going to turn into your bitter old mother. I'm the best thing ever happened to you. You better treat me right, girl. No one else will have you.*

I lifted the ax off the carpet and yanked the blanket away, ready to swing all over again, but the sight of him stopped me—the glistening red stain under his neck where the first strike had hit, the second across his ear when he had turned from a dead sleep.

He always slept soundly after sex. It was easier to let him have his way and hope he finished quickly.

The third and fourth gash dug into his cheek and nose. His eyes were still wide open, staring at me. I covered him again and leaned across the bed.

What if he was right about me? I hadn't ever really been alone. I'd gone straight from my parent's house to my husband's.

People had thought me pretty once, in high school. At least some boys did. I smiled at the thought of Robbie. He was smart, kind, broad-shouldered—better looking than Ethan in many ways, but he lacked Ethan's passion, his fire. Robbie never challenged me. He was a simple, uncomplicated man. Even after I broke his heart, Robbie once said I could call him anytime, and he would be there for me. I wondered if I could still call on him.

Robbie had graduated college and married Cindy Brown. I heard they had a second child on the way. I wondered what it must be like to live such a quiet, predictable life. The only thing predictable in my life had been the constant battle.

Robbie's life had moved forward. Ethan and I hadn't changed much since high school, especially Ethan. He was still tall, still firm-bodied. My pale skin now sank under my cheek bones. Creases had formed around my eyes, and frown lines blemished my mouth. Ethan was right. Who would want me now?

The stack of bills lay on the floor where I had dropped them. Without Ethan, I had no way of making the house payment. Between our parents' combined gifts, this house had almost been paid off after our wedding, but Ethan, financial wizard that he was, decided to take out a second mortgage to finance that showy pickup truck which he got totaled a few weeks later.

I spun around, facing the open bedroom door. "It *was too* your fault it got wrecked! I never would have driven off in your precious truck if you hadn't been drinking!"

I waited, but the lump didn't fight back, didn't point out that we were already home when I had driven off or that I had been drinking too.

"But not as much!" I insisted.

Ethan remained motionless. The house was too silent. I crawled next to the lump and clung to it as I had the night before, wiping my tears on the blanket covering him. I hated Ethan, but I hated myself more for missing him.

I would show him. I would make it look like a break-in. The burglars hadn't known Ethan was home, got freaked out and killed him.

You idiot! They killed me with my own ax? And what did you do while they were in here killing me?

He was right. I had to get rid of the ax, and I couldn't have been home when it happened. Although Peterman had already seen me, Ethan hadn't been dead long. I could go to my sister's, stay for a few days. No one would know exactly when the killing took place.

They'll find out. All they have to do is talk to the neighbors about how we screamed at each other every night.

"You're forgetting the most important part," I said to the lump. "No one cares enough about you to investigate. No one cares because *you* are a jerk!"

I was breathing hard. Everything was so quiet. A neighbor's car started and drove away.

I called my sister and told her I would be coming. She was too ecstatic to notice the tremor in my voice, or perhaps she just ignored it. I hadn't talked to her in a year... since the last time I had tried to leave Ethan.

I crammed clothes into a small bag. Then I realized I needed to take some stuff if I wanted it to look like we had been robbed.

What would a burglar take? What did we have worth stealing? I stuffed random things into a suitcase, including a $300 immersion blender. Would burglars steal expensive kitchen appliances? I didn't know.

A true genius at work.

"Be quiet!" I snatched a ceramic mug off the counter and whizzed it across the room. After a short pause, I motioned at the dented drywall and shattered mug. "As usual, I have to clean everything up!"

The back door creaked as I peeked out. The sun cast cool shade behind the house. Green grass grew in patches within our faded privacy fence. Dogs barked in the distance. A lawnmower buzzed at the end of the street. The world was going on as if nothing had changed. I crept outside, confident no one was looking, and lifted the ax.

The bedroom window didn't tinkle like I expected, but instead made a loud snap, followed by the soft clatter of fragments hitting the carpet within. I waited to see if anyone would pop out and ask about the noise, but no one appeared, so I knocked some more glass away, making a larger hole.

"Joanie, what are you doing?"

"My name is Joanne!"

Something moved in the shadowy room behind the broken glass. "Shut up, you idiot! Clean up this mess!"

Ethan looked out at me, cheek split open to his ear, nose hanging loose. "And get me some aspirin."

My knees buckled. I fell back in the grass and stared up at him. I didn't think to ask how he was still alive or consider what he might do if he realized what I had done to him. I hated him for being alive, but I hated myself more because I was relieved to have him back.

Now, things could finally go back to normal.

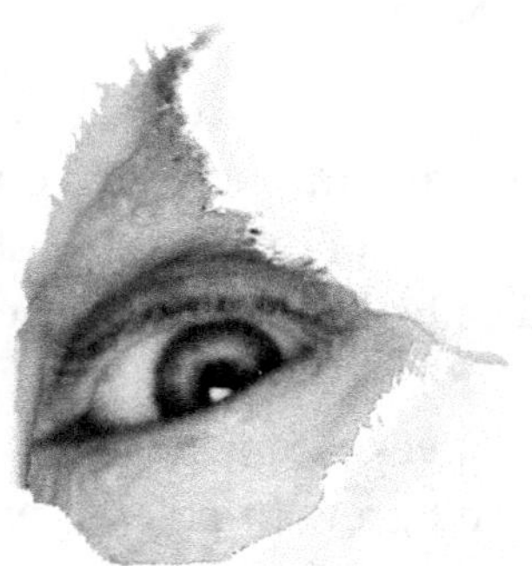

MAN EATER

The semi was gone, of course, by the time I arrived on the scene. Twenty-four hours after the body was discovered, life had returned to normal, at least for the customers. For most of these people, the Travel Stop was just a quick pause for gas, bathroom and food while passing though Albuquerque on their way somewhere else. Showers were available for truckers and campers as well.

Customers of the Travel Stop had no reason to watch the local news or read the local paper. They had no idea a murder had taken place, but the smell still lingered. Amid the diesel fumes and hot pavement, I could tell you exactly where the truck had been parked. The spot remained empty. The truckers avoided it as though it was haunted. The employees were more solemn than usual with none of the banter I might expect. Most were reluctant to talk, but they filled in a few details.

A white baseball cap protected the delicate, pink scalp under my thinning hair from the harsh New Mexico sun. I thought the hat made the brown ponytail hanging over my shoulders much less classy, but sunburns and skin cancer were a harsh reality. It was a little warm for a jacket, but my khaki sport coat concealed a pistol and shoulder holster. I hadn't needed my Beretta subcompact in two and a half years, but I felt vulnerable without its comforting weight.

As a private investigator, I spent a lot of time in my car and entertained myself by listening to the local radio. This story had gotten my attention: *John Hall found torn to pieces in his truck as though ripped to shreds by a pack of dogs.* That had been the DJ's exact words, but the victim's family said he didn't own a dog, and dogs don't politely shut the door behind them when they leave the sleeper behind the cab of your truck.

The land around the travel stop was flat for miles. The Sandia Mountains looked close, but they were over an hour's drive east. A large animal would have nowhere to run unless it crawled into someone else's vehicle.

Dogs aren't the only things with claws and teeth. I don't like to talk about my missing nine years. I had been gone—not just out of town gone. I had become something other than human, an animal. Then one day, with no seeming rhyme or reason, I was back. Rebuilding my life had been a constant struggle. At night, when I am alone with my thoughts, I fear I might change again and never return.

If there was someone else like me out there, they might be responsible for this murder. Maybe they could explain what had happened to me and ensure it never happened again… or maybe they would destroy everything I'd managed to rebuild. Either way, I needed to know.

My faded, forest-green station wagon chugged south through downtown Albuquerque. I'd had a fair amount of success recently and finally paid off my debts. Soon, I'd have enough money for a new car, but for now, the wagon still got me where I needed to go… most of the time. It had spent a fair amount of time in the shop recently.

The AC didn't work, but the open windows brought in a breeze of dry, dusty air, and the smells of the world came in with it. Fryer grease congealed in a recycling bin behind a fast food joint. Animal urine marked a tree at the corner. A squirrel decomposed on the side of the road two blocks away.

I knew Daryl's daily wandering took him past the Price Rite and, sure enough, I found him in the garbage behind the store, rooting around for food.

"Score!" he said, pulling out a whole loaf of barely expired bread.

"I think they throw it out for you on purpose," I said.

"Jack!" He leapt down and rolled his back on the hard blacktop, exposing a bit of belly through his bright yellow T-shirt.

"You don't need to do that."

"How else can I show you I'm no threat?"

I shook my head, smiling. I couldn't see this skinny, malnourished wreck in ill-fitting clothes as a threat, but perhaps I should have been more wary. There was more to him than met the eye. We had been in the same militant cult together. I'd thought I was the only one to survive their experiment until Daryl tracked me down. He was alive, but not quite all there. Hell, maybe I wasn't altogether sane myself.

He didn't smell as bad as you might expect, and I detected a hint of shampoo. He must have showered at the shelter that morning.

He rolled upright, still crouching. "Are Meega and Alpha here?"

"No, I didn't bring the dogs."

He frowned.

"Did you hear what happened at the Travel Stop?" I asked.

He cocked his head. "What happened?"

"A truck driver was killed. Police say he was torn apart by an animal. You ever make it out that far?"

He stood and faced me. "You know I don't. Unless you drive me." His mouth hung open. "You can't possibly think I did it!"

I didn't answer.

"I thought you came by to visit…" He shook his head and backed away. "You just came to accuse me of-of-of—" His back slid down against the cinderblock wall, and he banged the back of his head against the bricks. It was difficult to remember this man once spoke three languages and used to beat us all at Monopoly.

I dropped to one knee and grabbed him. "No! Come on. I know you didn't do it. You could never hurt someone." But I didn't know. Not really. "I just wanted to ask if you'd heard anything and to make sure you were safe. You're more connected to the streets than I am. You doin' good?"

He beamed a great big smile of yellowed teeth. "I'm doing great, Jack!" He got on all fours and peered under the trash bin. "You hear that?"

"What?"

"A big, juicy rat! If you go around the other side and flush him out, I'll split him with you!"

I winced. "You don't have to eat rats, Daryl. Let me buy you a sandwich."

"But I like rats. Besides, sandwiches don't run."

As strange as Daryl might seem, I hadn't been much different once. Yes, I'd eaten raw rats and even garbage when the dogs and I couldn't find a squirrel or rabbit to share. I tried not to think about it, let alone discuss it. Even my best friend, Diane, had no idea what I'd been through. How could she even believe it, let alone understand? I was lucky to have climbed as far up the ladder back to humanity as I had, but I still had quite a ways to go, and I didn't truly understand all that Catalyst had done to us.

Once we finished our sandwiches, I told Daryl I needed to leave, but he kept asking questions and repeating stories, trying to get me to stay.

Once I had finally freed myself from Daryl, I made my way to the New Mexico Scientific Laboratories building. Dr. Kakali Bhatia kept the thick, dark hair circling her soft, round face short, possibly to keep it from dangling into dead people's guts, but I didn't like to think about that.

We'd met a few times when I had been working cases, and I was familiar enough to her that she brought me downstairs. Antiseptics and bleach could not cover the smell of cold meat. She unzipped John Hall's black body bag. His glassy eyes stared straight up as though focusing on some invisible terror in the ceiling.

Dr. Bhatia pointed out the torn neck. "That's what killed him." She then pointed out the irregular gaps in the man's bloodied gut.

I backed away to keep from vomiting. "The murderer… ate pieces of him?"

"Not murder. An animal did this. No man has a mouth wide enough or strong enough to do that to his neck. At least the end wasn't all unpleasant for him."

"What do you mean?"

She lowered the zipper further, revealing the man's crotch.

"Oh! My!" Beyond the blood and the intestinal contents, I now detected the fading musk of passion.

"Just like the other one," she said.

"Other one?"

"A travelling salesman found mauled behind the I-40 rest stop east of town a few days ago. Almost the same injuries and the same…" she motioned down with her head.

"You can zip him up now," I said. "Is that normal?"

"Men do sometimes lose control of their functions during a traumatic death. There can be a rush of endorphins. Some claim it makes death less painful, but I think that's just something people say to make themselves feel better. I thought the first victim had been killed by a bear down from the Sandia Mountains, but a bear could never make it as far as the Travel Stop, at least not on its own, and John Hall was killed with one bite to the neck from a strong, wide mouth, not the way bears kill. My friend from the zoo thinks it looks like a tiger or lion attack."

"A tiger…? Or a bear…? Did the circus come through town?" I felt strangely better. Daryl and I were off the hook. This wasn't *my* concern. This was a job for animal control.

My phone rang and Luis, my boss, asked me if I'd gotten any good photos. He'd assigned me to watch Billie Jean DeChant's house. Her employer suspected her of faking an injury to get worker's comp and wanted us to catch her doing jumping jacks or painting her house or whatever, revealing she was secretly healthy. My job is so glamorous.

I winced. "Not yet. I'm on it."

"Don't tell me you haven't even started!"

"I just stepped away for a few minutes!"

"Jack! I've seen what you are capable of when you are on your game. I don't have to tell you that when you step away is when all the stuff you need to photograph happens! Do you want me to assign someone else to this case?"

I wanted to say yes, but of course I couldn't. "No! I'm on it!"

If I backed out of the Billie Jean case, Luis was likely to stop hiring me. I only got paid per job, and I needed the work. These days, Luis is more of a marketer than an investigator himself. If you needed a PI in Albuquerque, Luis Navarro was likely the first name you think of. He had so many clients that he farmed work to other PI's. I liked to think I was a decent investigator, but nobody knew my name.

On my way to Billie Jean's, I stopped by my studio apartment to walk the dogs. I think they were the reason I hadn't ended up like Daryl. I belonged to a pack, and we relied on each other.

I parked the wagon cattycorner from Billie Jean's single level ranch in a tightly packed subdivision. My telephoto lens was ready for her, but she didn't show her face. I knew she was home though. Her car was in the driveway, and someone had dragged the trash to the curb since I had taken my break. As Luis had said, a perfect photograph opportunity had been missed.

The radio caught my attention again with more breaking news, another animal attack at a motel in Kingman, Arizona.

My mind reeled. It couldn't be a coincidence, and what wild animal sneaks inside a closed motel room? Could the victim have left the door open, allowing a stray to creep inside?

I whipped out my laptop from under the seat and started Googling the three victims, trying to find some connection between them: A truck driver, a salesman, a family man. They lived in different cities, grew up in different towns. One didn't go to college, while the other two went to different ones. I didn't find any connection, but I found something else, a fourth animal attack in the back seat of a car in East Saint Louis. I broadened my search and discovered another man had been torn apart at a rest stop outside of Terre Haute, Indiana, and another in Oklahoma. I found other attacks as well, mostly around Pennsylvania. They didn't all fit the pattern and may not have been related. Some were in alleyways, hunting trips in the woods, barns, even inside suburban houses. Not all the details were listed online, even on the more inclusive databases I had access too, but a few phone calls confirmed the most recent killings matched the basic description: animals attacking male travelers in a state of sexual arousal.

I wondered why no one else had linked the killings. They were assumed to be somewhat random animal attacks. They were unusual, but must not have sent up the red flags authorities look for. With the body count rising however, others were bound to make the same connection I had.

Whether the murderer was a person, animal, or supernatural creature, they were begging to be caught, and they'd crossed state lines. If it hadn't been already, the case would be assigned to the FBI. They would either kill the creature or drive it underground, along with any potential revelations about what Catalyst had turned me into.

I phoned Diane, Luis' office manager and my most trusted friend other than the dogs. "Something's come up. Can you put someone else on the Billie Jean case?"

"I'm not in the office today, Jack. You're going to have to call Luis."

"You're not…" Diane almost never took a day off. I'd much rather deal with her than Luis. He would give me grief and possibly a lecture. I could already hear him: *Your problem, Jack, is that you let yourself get bored and your mind wanders to cases that look more interesting to you, but interesting doesn't pay the bills.*

I pressed on with Diane. "I guess that means you probably aren't available to watch the dogs tonight."

"Nope. Sorry."

"Are you sure? I really need to take care of something."

"The world doesn't revolve around you, Jack. I've got a life too!"

"Of course! I know. Sorry. That was stupid of me. I've got other people I can ask. You deserve some time off."

"Hell yeah, I do!"

"I don't suppose Reece…?"

"He's nine, Jack! If you really want to ask him, I can give you my ex-husband's phone number. That's who he's staying with."

"No! No, that's alright. Enjoy your time off."

I deserved every bit of frustration I felt from Diane that day, but she was usually more patient with my thoughtlessness.

"Wait," I said. "Is something wrong?"

"I'm fine."

"A wise person once told me that no man is an island. I assume that goes for women too."

I could hear a smile return to her voice. "So, you actually do listen to me, even if you never take my advice. I just need some time off, Jack. I'm going to spend a couple days with my sister."

"You've got my number if you need anything."

"I know. Thanks, Jack."

I held the phone for a moment even though she had hung up. She'd done so much for me since I had returned to civilization. I wished there was more I could do for her, but she wasn't letting me in. Now I knew how she felt when I couldn't share the strange details of my dark history and past acquaintances.

I called the one other person in town I trusted. When he said no, I was tempted to ask Luis, but not only did I expect he would say no, I couldn't imagine him as an attentive caretaker. He'd probably let my dogs starve. I had grown to rely on Diane and her son far more than I liked to admit. Between the two of them, I always had reliable dog-sitters, along with Diane's ear and guidance. Perhaps she would eventually let me return the favor.

I imagined the killer's trail getting cold as I watched Billie Jean's house and waited for a chance photograph that would probably never happen. Whoever or whatever had killed those people was getting further away, along with possible answers about my own horrific transformations.

* * *

I found Daryl socializing outside the homeless shelter. When I asked him to take care of the dogs, he jumped with excitement.

He sat the bag of groceries on the floor of my studio apartment and let little Alpha lick his face. The larger dog, Meega, looked up at me questioningly, as if to ask, "Are you seriously leaving us with this guy?"

Daryl reached into the grocery sack. "Let's see what we have to eat!"

"No!" I put the bag on the counter in the attached kitchenette. "Only dog food and treats for them. Groceries are for *you*."

Daryl popped a dog treat in his mouth and chewed. "Eh, they're okay I guess. Hot dogs are better."

I gave Daryl a prepaid cell phone. "I'll call you three times a day with updates."

Daryl saluted. "You can trust me, Jack! I won't let my pack down!"

I winced. This was *my* pack. Not his. I pushed the flash of irrational jealousy out of my mind. I was lucky to have Daryl's help.

* * *

A faded, decades old sign read, *The Byway Motel, now with color TV in every room!*

Yellow tape still barred the second story outdoor entrance to the motel room in Kingman. A maid unlocked the door and let me examine the blood-soaked mattress and smell the animal musk. The police had already removed all the victim's belongings. Yesterday, Gerald Oates had dropped his freshman daughter off at Northern Arizona University. This morning, a maid found him dead on the bed without his pants.

No possessions or credit cards were reported missing, but there was no cash either.

Moisture clung to the bottom of the tiny motel bathtub in the harsh florescent light. Little shampoo and conditioner bottles sat empty on the edge. I reached into the drain and pulled out a clump of dark black hair. Mr. Oates' hair was short and peppered with gray. Had the police even considered that the animal who did this might have showered before they left? Or did the maid service just not clean the rooms very well between guests in this two star motel?

I spread the map over the hood of the wagon and plotted the attacks in reverse chronological order starting here at the Byway Motel. The attacks followed an unmistakable path westward. Kingman's entire economy was based on the intersection of highways, and lay less than an hour from both California and Nevada. Which path would the killer take from here?

I had gotten closer, at an actual crime scene the same day as the murder. I didn't want to just wait for the killer to strike again. Would they continue following historic Route 66 into California? Where in these three states would lions, tigers or bears call home?

* * *

It seemed every surface was coated in flashing light bulbs, but the effect wasn't quite as impressive in the late afternoon sun. I walked up the Vegas strip past lines of people slapping flyers in an attempt to get my attention as they handed out cards promoting clubs and entertainers. This gambling Mecca was one part amusement park and one part adult fantasy land.

I made it to the Mirage hotel and casino just after the public tiger feeding had started. Fascinated kids and adults watched the gold and white striped beasts tear into horse carcasses donated by area farmers. The largest cat had paws bigger than my face. I witnessed firsthand what their dagger-sized canines and massive claws could do to flesh.

A boyish Asian man in safari garb gave rehearsed tiger trivia as the animals ate. Once the crowd dispersed I was able to talk to him.

"I'm looking for someone who owns a large cat and travelled with it recently."

"Well, honey, you came to the right town. You'd be surprised how many people have tigers around Vegas. It's not just magicians and performers. Club owners, gangsters, eccentric rich people— they think owning a tiger makes them look like big shots. Can you say *overcompensating?*"

I frowned as the suspect list grew.

The man mistook my expression. "Don't be sad! We take good care of the animals here. They get rotated in from a big habitat outside the city where they got all kinds of room to play." He looked into the enclosure and shook his head. "Most people don't realize what they're getting into when they buy a wild animal. They can hurt the animal or get themselves hurt."

I struggled to find the right words as I watched the beasts chew away flesh. "Have these animals killed people?"

"Well, not *these* animals," he said waving toward the tigers. "But accidents do happen. These creatures don't show love the same ways we do, and we are way more fragile than other tigers."

"So they *can* love a human?"

"They can be very loving and protective, but, like I said, that kind of affection can be more dangerous than indifference. You aren't thinking of buying one are you?"

I laughed. "Oh, no! My two dogs and I barely fit in my apartment as it is!" I paused. "Could you train tigers to kill?"

"To kill a person? Well, I suppose, but it would be pretty dangerous. If they were trained to think it's ok to kill humans, they might just attack their trainers."

"So you've never heard of it happening?"

"Golly, no! You are a morbid one, ain't you?"

"Just curious. They are such beautiful creatures." I considered my words. "Could you fake being a tiger, like with fake jaws and claws?"

The man grinned broadly, looking even more boyish. "Oh, I see what you are getting at. You don't need to play coy, Mister. Anything goes in Vegas, if you find the right people. You like to dress up?"

"Me? No! But… possibly someone else—"

He nodded. "Oh, I got you covered." He pulled out a flyer and handed it to me. "You can find almost anything in Vegas."

I looked at a digitally enhanced photo of a scantily clad cat-woman. It read, *Sister Slash appearing for a limited time at Marigold Sky! Once in a lifetime Feline fun! Meow!*

I felt my face getting warm. "No, this isn't—"

The man winked. "Don't be embarrassed. Cat fetishes aren't as uncommon as you might think. That's not half as freaky as some of the things people ask me about. I hear the girl on that flyer will do all kinds of crazy stuff for the right price."

I didn't have any better leads to follow while I waited for another victim to die. I stuffed the card in my pocket. "Thanks."

"Tell 'em Johnny from the Mirage sent you!"

* * *

The sun set as I pulled off Dean Martin Drive and my faded green wagon rolled to a stop behind a polished limo. I called out to the valet service. "Where can I park?"

"We'll park it for you."

"I'd rather park it myself."

"It's complimentary. No public parking in this lot."

I groaned and reluctantly gave up my keys. My laptop and tablet were stashed under the seat, and I needed them for my job. At least they were password protected.

"Careful," I said as I tossed over my keys. "She's temperamental."

Glass doors opened into a narrow hallway and muffled music. A large, suited man stood next to a counter. "No guns allowed inside the club, sir." He straightened, but didn't seem overly tense or upset. "You can check your gun at the counter."

I examined my khaki jacket and unbuckled the shoulder holster, wondering how he had spotted it so easily. He tied a numbered tag to the gun and gave me a slip of paper with the same number.

"Admission is twenty-five dollars and I need to see some ID."

I sighed and obliged. A big sign read, *Absolutely no photographs allowed; management reserves right to remove anyone from premises for any reason.*

"Thank you," the man said. "Have a good time."

My attention was immediately drawn to three stages and what looked like bored dancers in different stages of undress. One leaned against a pole in the middle of the stage, while another held a pole in one hand as she sauntered around it. In booths lining the mirrored walls, dancers laughed with men in suits. Faces remained shadowy in the dim, colored lights. Perhaps I shouldn't have been surprised to see three female spectators amid the faces, still far outnumbered by the men.

I practically walked into a waitress carrying a tray of drinks. "Whoa! Sorry!"

"I'm used to it. What can I get you?"

"Nothing, thanks."

I was about to ask about the cat-woman I'd seen on the flyer, but the waitress spoke first. "There's a two drink minimum."

I sighed again and ordered a beer. She slipped through the crowd before I could ask my question.

Loud voices drew my attention away from the stages. The yelling became loud enough to overpower the music. A young, blond man, probably barley into his twenties, shoved a gangly man in an oversized suit. Long, greasy hair tumbled over the skinny man's shoulders.

"That's not a woman!" the clean-cut boy shouted. "I want my money back!"

"No refunds!" the greasy man responded.

"I probably need a rabies shot!"

"Joey!" The greasy man hollered.

The bouncer from the doorway calmly lifted the blond boy from the ground and shoved him toward the exit. As they made their way to the door, I noticed four rips in the back of the boy's jacket, and a hint of blood.

"I'll sue your asses off!" The boy screamed. "I'll get your permits revoked—shut you down!"

The greasy man followed with a smug smile. "Big talk! I'd like to see you try!"

Joey put a hand out, blocking the greasy man from following. "Don't make things worse, T-Bone."

"This isn't over!" the boy screamed as Joey pushed him out the door. The crowd applauded as though it were all part of a show.

The waitress brought my beer. "You want to run a tab?"

"I'll pay as I go." I motioned my chin toward the door. "Does that happen often?"

She shrugged. "Comes with the territory."

I scanned the nametag on her bulging, low-cut blouse. "Cherry? Is that your real name?"

"It is tonight."

I smiled. "How long have you worked here, Cherry?"

"Almost a year."

"What can you tell me about the cat-woman?"

"Tips have never been better since she showed up a few weeks ago."

Before I could ask another question, Cherry was gone again, clearing glasses and waiting on more customers.

The song ended, and all three girls left the stage. A voice boomed across the room. "Thank our ladies for their service! But now it's time for the woman you've all come to see. You'll never see another like… Sister Slash!"

Something leapt up into the steel rafters where the lights and speakers were suspended. Percussion bled into a driving electric guitar which filled the room with anticipation. She swung down, caught the metal pole on the center stage and spiraled around until she landed on all fours with her head low. Slitted eyes stared straight into my face while Janet Jackson sang 'Black Cat' over the speakers. Medium-length, black hair sloped into a widow's peak above thick, dark eyebrows, and faded freckles graced the tops of her cheeks.

I felt paralyzed, like prey holding the gaze of an alpha predator who would chase me if I ran. She smiled, revealing white, needle-like teeth.

The tension immediately left me when she said, "Hello," in a light, airy voice.

She back flipped away and caught the eyes of a man on the other side of the stage, exactly as she had mine, with her chest low and her butt in the air. A tail curled above tight vinyl pants. She arched backwards and caught the pole with one hand. Silver buckles held three matching vinyl bras over the six breasts on her torso. The pair on top appeared fuller and rounder than the others.

I'd heard of some wild plastic surgeries, like a woman who wanted to look like Barbie, and I only had to look behind me to see exaggerated breast implants, but I'd never imagined anything like this. The crowd loved it. Well, most of them did.

Dollars fell over the stage. She tried to catch the eye of a young black man sitting at the stage across from me, but he backed away, laughing. His friend, however, waved money in the air and was more than happy to let the animal woman lick his face and rub her six breasts against him while his friend shook his head and laughed. I got the impression he laughed to cover shock and nervousness rather than from actual amusement.

Slash swished her hips to the driving beat. She spun on the pole with her body at a rigid ninety degrees, then pulled herself against the polished steel and held herself upside down with nothing but the strength of her thighs.

I stared, mesmerized, as she rotated slowly, giving us all a good look while the crowd cheered and the dollars fell. When she released her thighs, she fell rapidly, and I gasped, thinking for sure she would bust her head on the stage, but she flipped back once more onto her hands and knees. She crawled toward me, and her lip curled upward. Lights sparkled in her bright green eyes. She pulled me forward by my jacket lapel.

"I-I…" My mouth was dry and I stuttered in a rare moment of speechlessness. "I don't have any money."

She cocked her head, pursed her lips, and turned her attention to the man two chairs away from me. She eyed me, making sure I was seeing what I was missing.

I stood up from the stage and turned away, wiping the sweat from my forehead with the sleeve of my jacket.

I hadn't been to a strip club since basic training, and I'd certainly never been to one like Marigold Sky. I was getting an adult education tonight.

As the song ended, the crowd gasped, and I turned in time to see her leaping over men's heads and landing on the far stage, where she did a much slower routine, working the crowd and making conversation over the 'Stray Cat Strut' by the Stray Cats. I now understood why the other dancers had left their posts. This was now Slash's show, and she owned all three stages.

Barely noticed, T-Bone, the greasy man I had seen kicking the frat boy out, now swept bills from the center stage into a bag.

Slash picked up the beat again with Poison's 'Look What the Cat Dragged In.' When the song ended, three new girls strutted onto the stages to begin their dances. I pushed though the crowd while Slash scooped up bills and spoke to members of the audience.

"Can I talk to you?" I asked.

"I'll be available for private dances in the back."

The dancer who now shared the stage with Slash scowled down at her and made a fake, angry cat noise, "Reowr!"

Slash stood up and hissed at her. For a moment, I thought she might be capable of the type of violence that had taken place at the Kingman motel or the Travel Stop.

T-Bone confronted the other performer. "Play nice with your star!"

"She's not a star! She's a freak show taking all the tips!"

It appeared while the waitresses had seen an increase in their tips, the other dancers weren't as happy about the new headliner.

The man told Slash to "Go on back," while the woman continued to taunt her, saying, "You better run!"

Slash's nails sprouted a full inch from the tips of her fingers.

The man slapped the stage. "I said back!"

Slash pouted out her lips and retreated into the dressing rooms. I tried to follow, but T-Bone barred my way.

"Only performers allowed back there," he said.

"She said we could talk."

"Private dances are 200 dollars."

"200?" I looked longingly past T-Bone toward the dressing rooms. This woman was certainly not like me or Daryl, but she was part animal. She might know others. She might have answers.

T-Bone must have mistaken the look on my face. "I can see you are really taken with our special girl. You're not like the other guys who come in here. I like you. 150 gets you some alone time with the woman of your fantasies."

I thought about my new car fund and my new apartment fund. "I don't know. That's still a lot of money." I briefly considered waiting behind the building for her to get off her shift, but that was a surefire way to get kicked off the property or possibly arrested.

"You'll never find another like her," T-Bone said. "It's a once in a lifetime experience."

"I only have 95 dollars in my wallet."

T-Bone shook his head and smiled, revealing a large gap in his teeth. "I must be crazy, but I don't want you to miss this, buddy." He directed me into a dimly lit room about the size of a closet and onto the waiting mini-couch within. "She'll be with you in a minute." A curtain fell closed, muffling the music outside.

From T-Bone's smile, I could tell he thought he had a fish on his line. After one taste, I'd be at the ATM, ready to spend all my money. Little did T-Bone know how little money I had. The thought was comforting, however. If they saw me as an investment, Slash was less likely to tear me to pieces or eat me. Even if she was a killer, she couldn't hurt me here. She'd be out of a job.

The minutes ticked by, and I wondered if they had taken my money and run. I doubted it though. That would put them in bad with the club owners, and they wouldn't want to lose this steady gig.

The curtain finally jerked open. Red light silhouetted a willowy body. Clawed hands worked down her front, unbuckling the vinyl top.

"Hello," I said. "My name is Jack, I was wondering if we could talk…"

She pounced onto my lap with hands and feet balanced on my thighs. Cotton candy perfume filled my nostrils. Her fingernails caught on my pants and poked the skin within. I thought about how deadly those nails could be. They weren't even fully protracted.

She nudged my neck with her nose. I recoiled, laughing with more than a bit of fear as well as surprise. I hadn't been touched in this way for quite some time and was more ticklish than I remembered. Before I knew what was happening, she had pushed me forward enough that she could slide her warm, soft body behind me, then wrap around me like she had the pole out front. Her spine curved in ways I'd never seen. Her tail curled playfully behind her while a purr rumbled and vibrated deep within her chest.

"No petting," she whispered. "That costs extra."

I'm embarrassed to admit I almost asked how much extra.

Her tongue was rougher than expected when it ran up my cheek, like wet sandpaper, and her breath smelled like slightly soured milk, but not in a bad way. Behind the sickly sweet perfume, I detected a sensual musk. I tried to maintain my composure, but she could see my arousal.

"There it is…" she said.

"I'm just here to talk." By now I knew this was more than some exotic plastic surgery fetish. This was all her. "How did you get like this?"

"I've always been this way." She spread out, arching her back against my lap, displaying her six breasts and plump, pink nipples. "You like?"

"Yes." I was surprised to hear myself say it. "Yes I do."

"You'll never find another like me."

I swallowed hard. "Are you sure? Were your… parents like this?"

She stiffened and sat up suddenly. "What kind of freak are you?"

"I'm different too. I might be able to understand in ways others can't, and maybe you'll have some answers for me too!"

She stood up and buckled her top back on. "This is over."

"No! Wait! I might be able to help you!"

"I don't need no white knight! I've got all the help I need."

I tried to follow her out, but T-Bone blocked my path while she rushed back to the dressing rooms.

"You causing trouble?" T-Bone asked? "Is this how you repay my kindness?"

"I told you, I just want to talk."

"Well, you said the wrong thing. Plenty other dancers here you can *talk* to." With that he followed in the direction of his star.

A scream briefly overpowered the music. A frantic stripper emoted and gesticulated to the DJ. The music broke off, but began again. Joey, the bouncer, darted from his post and made for the dressing rooms. The performers paused their routines, looking for some explanation. Slash emerged, but T-Bone grabbed her arm and pulled her back out of sight.

I followed into the now unguarded dressing room. I ignored the primping performers and found an open back door.

Joey stood in the alley with another man and held a phone in his hand. Other performers had begun to gather. Propped against a brick wall, the blond boy who had threatened trouble earlier now lay on the pavement with his throat ripped out. He stared ahead with wide, open eyes. He had been looking at his attacker when he died.

I spotted a security camera above the door. The body lay exactly in the camera's blind spot. No animal had done this. The killer had known exactly what they were doing.

Joey still had the phone in one hand when he announced, "We're closing up for the night."

"You can't close!" one of the performers argued. "Marigold Sky never closes!"

A brunette woman darted from nowhere. From her capris and tank top, I knew she wasn't one of the performers. "Ashley!" she called, waving. "Ashley, wait!"

T-Bone pushed Slash into the passenger seat of a bright orange Camaro and peeled away.

The brunette chased the Camaro, waving her arms in the air, and I followed close behind. As the car pulled further away, the woman turned suddenly and blocked my path.

"What do you want with Ashley?"

"Ashley?"

"You call her Slash."

The widow's peak, green eyes and musky scent all came together for me, even though this young woman was clearly no animal. "You're related! Are you her… sister?"

"Yes. That agent of hers won't let me talk to her. Everyone wants to control her, to take advantage. So, again I ask, what do you want with my sister?"

"I just want to talk to her. I think we might be able to help each other."

"You're not the first boy to use that line on her."

"She's in big trouble. Did she kill that man?"

"My sister would never do that!"

"Maybe not, but she'll be the first suspect, and there's more, a string of dead men from here to Pennsylvania."

She crossed her arms, and thick eyebrows came together over-deep set eyes.

"If I can talk to her before the police find her, maybe I can help. I know what it's like to feel out of control, to be driven by instincts you don't understand. It's like a kind of temporary insanity."

She focused on me. "Maybe you do understand. Have you had dinner?"

"No!" I said, not believing my luck. I might not be able to get the truth directly from Slash, but I might get the next best thing.

"Great," she said. "You're buying. You have a car?"

* * *

My new friend Irene and I settled into a booth in a cheap buffet at a casino down the street. The way she tore into the roast chicken made me wonder when she had last eaten. I hadn't eaten all day myself. We got my money's worth.

"Life was never easy for Ashley," Irene said through mouthfuls of food. "Before puberty, she could hide her deformity, but then it became impossible."

"Is it a deformity?"

"What would you call it? She started seeking attention, any attention. Aunt Sara even tried locking her in her room to keep her out of trouble, but she ran off with the first guy who was nice to her. It's a cliché, right?"

"That's how she met T-Bone?"

"Oh, hell no. The first guy was just some small-time dealer—a wannabe pimp. He broke her heart, traded her off to someone else, and then, finally, she ended up with T-Bone. He had more ambition than the rest and dragged her down here."

"They traded her? You make her sound like property!"

"That's all she is to them—a commodity. Everyone wants to control her."

"She looked pretty in control on stage."

Irene narrowed her eyes and cracked a chicken bone to suck the marrow. "Looks can be deceiving."

"So she was born like that then—part cat? Do you have any idea how or why—?"

"She's not a cat! She's my sister!"

"Of course! Poor choice of words. Is there anyone else in the family like her?"

"I wouldn't know. Shortly after she was born, our parents left us with Aunt Sara, and I never saw them again. I used to blame Ashley for causing Mom and Dad to abandon us... to abandon me. I was only two years old when they left!" She shook her head. "I used to wish she'd never been born." Irene paused for a moment. "Now I see that if I had treated Ashley better, maybe she wouldn't have gone looking for affection in all the wrong places."

I nodded, disappointed. If there were others like Slash—Ashley—neither sister appeared to have any knowledge of them. They were as lost as I was, probably more so.

Irene grabbed my hand from across the table. "I have to find her! I have to explain how wrong I was. Together, the two of us can be unbeatable!"

I nodded. "Marigold Sky is closed, at least for tonight. T-Bone and Slash are in the wind. They won't be back, at least not until the dust has settled, and even then, the club might see them as a liability."

"I got so close, but so far away."

"Maybe we can still find her. I'm a private investigator."

She pulled her hand away. "Who hired you?"

"No one. This is personal. I feel like I identify with your sister a little bit."

"It doesn't matter. She's lost."

"Maybe not."

"You can really find her?"

"Are you hiring me?"

"I don't have money." She moved into the booth with me, and ran a finger through my thinning hair. "Maybe I can find another way to repay you?"

Surprised, I caught her hand and gently pulled it away from my face. "I can't go for that. For one thing, I'm not licensed in Nevada, anyway."

"So you won't help?"

"I didn't say that."

"In my experience, men never give you anything unless they think they are getting something in return."

"I told you, this is personal for me. If I can understand your sister, maybe I can understand myself."

The corner of her mouth rose, and she leaned her face close to mine. "That's sweet." I could smell the chicken grease on her lips. "If you are going to help anyway, then why not take what you want from me?"

This woman was like a human, more socially acceptable version of the animal who had driven me so wild at the club. She even smelled the same. It had been so long since I had known a woman's touch. "I do want you," I admitted. "But I don't want you to do something because you think you have to, or because you want me to owe you."

She smiled and began to kiss me, gently at first, but then began gnawing on my lips, and working her way down my neck. I returned Irene's kisses and bumped the table as I embraced her, but secretly I was picturing her sister.

An old man dressed as a cowboy tipped his hat to me and winked. Irene and I both giggled.

"Do you have a room?" she asked.

In the bright lights I had forgotten how late it was. I stuttered out an answer, "Not yet. To be honest, I was planning on parking at one of the casinos and sleeping in my car, but I'll get one." I felt so unprofessional as she kissed my neck again, but Irene wasn't a client. This was my personal time, and my body needed this to happen.

She suddenly bit my chest, hard enough to leave a tiny mark the shape of her mouth.

"Ouch!"

She rose from the booth. "Not yet. I can't allow myself to feel pleasure until we find my sister. Then we can both relax. Then…" She touched my cheek. "I'm all yours."

I tried to regain my composure. She was most likely playing me, but it didn't matter. "I'll need as much info as you have on your sister and T-Bone. What are their full names?"

"You promise to bring me with you when look for them?"

I nodded.

"My sister's last name is Reed. T-Bone's real name is Eliot Thomas."

I continued to stare even after Irene disappeared into the flashing lights and ringing bells of the casino beyond.

Names were all I needed to begin my search, but Vegas is a transient city, and I didn't find any property or leases in Ashley or T-Bone's name. Neither of them had any social media presence either. Ashley didn't even have a savings account, but T-Bone had just purchased that shiny Camaro. I shook my head thinking of all the money falling over the stage tonight. There must have been over $1,000 for a single ten minute performance! A legitimate agent keeps ten percent, and I'm sure the club took a cut, but did T-Bone let Ashley keep anything at all for herself? T-Bone had a series of drug arrests and disorderlies on record, but nothing serious.

My new friend Irene Reed had enrolled in community college that year, but dropped out before finishing her first semester. I didn't find any record of them having an *Aunt Sara*. Perhaps she wasn't a blood relative. I found their parent's names. The father had died years ago of natural causes. The mother…

My breath caught in my throat. Their mother had been found dead in her kitchen… mauled by an animal little more than a week ago. All the other victims I had trailed across the country had been travelling men, but this couldn't be a coincidence.

* * *

T-Bone looked over his shoulder as he got out of the bright orange Camaro and crossed the street. Irene tensed in my passenger seat, prepared to pounce, but I grabbed her arm. "Not yet. We still don't know where your sister is. This is the address they listed on their Sheriff's cards and TAM cards. You need those to work as entertainers in Las Vegas, but they know this is the first place the police would look for them. They won't be staying here."

Irene crossed her arms. "So this is what private eyes do? Just sit and watch people?"

"Pretty much."

"You know, Aunt Sara never looked for Ashley after she ran away. She was probably relieved to be rid of her. Aunt Sara did the best she could, but she's not a rich girl. I don't think I ever saw Aunt Sara smile. We didn't come from privilege."

I grasped Irene's hand. "We'll find her."

"Can we listen to the radio or something?"

"Sure. Just keep the volume low."

In a couple minutes, T-Bone emerged with some bags, tossed them in his car and roared back onto the street.

I followed at a safe distance.

"You're going to lose him!" Irene shouted.

I smiled. "Relax. I'm not going to lose that bright orange car. Hell, if I lost sight of him, I could just listen for that engine."

Although I didn't think we'd left Las Vegas, a sign read *Enterprise, Nevada*. Houses were bordered by sidewalks and pebble beds with stubbly shrubs and palm trees.

An automatic gate opened in a seven foot stucco wall, and T-Bone pulled the Camaro inside. Pink clay roof tiles rose above the wall.

Irene unbuckled her seatbelt, and I grabbed her arm again.

"My sister is in there!" She said.

"But so is T-Bone and who knows who else! Trust me."

She let out a long breath and watched the automatic gate close. Sure enough, a few minutes later, the Camaro emerged again. T-Bone wasn't the type to hold still for long.

We slipped in the gate before it closed, marched up the arched portico and rang the doorbell.

A potbellied man in shorts and a Hawaiian shirt opened the door. Thinning silver hair parted over his head. "Did you forget your—?" He stopped abruptly when he saw us.

I could smell thick animal musk and raw meat within. "Hello. We're looking for Ashley Reed."

Irene had been patient as long as she could, and pushed her way past the man.

"Who are you?" he said. "I'm calling the police!"

"That's Ashley's sister. You might know Ashley as Slash."

"Sister!" he exclaimed. "Well, that's different! How exciting! Come in!"

I paused as I entered. In the front room sat a metal cage containing a lone tiger. It lazily gnawed on a giant femur using teeth large enough to tear out a man's throat in one bite.

"Don't mind Sonja," the man said. "The old girl wouldn't hurt a fly. My name's Harold. This is my house."

"Irene!" Ashley exclaimed from the living room. "What are you doing here?"

Ashley lazed on an L-shaped couch in front of a massive television. The table in front of her was littered with bottles, an empty ice cream carton, chips, and open pill bottles. She was beautiful, but far less sexualized in her long sleeve pajama top. An afghan covered her legs.

"I came to rescue you," Irene said.

"Do I look like I need saving?"

"Of course you do! You're being used… again!"

Ashley shook her head. "T-Bone takes care of me!"

"Isn't that what you said about Shane? And Weasel?"

Irene sat on the couch and grabbed her sister's hands. "I didn't understand before, but something's happened to me. I get it now! The only way for us to survive is together! You don't need T-Bone! You don't need any man! All we need is each other!"

Slash shook Irene's hands away. "You think you can just walk in and make everything right after all these years? You're no better than T-Bone or the others. You want to control me! At least T-Bone's honest about what he wants!"

A car engine revved out front.

"He's back!" Irene stood. "You have to come with me! Now!"

Ashley settled into the sofa. "Relax! Take a pill. Have something to drink."

T-Bone walked in and looked past me at the two women. "Step away from her!"

Irene bared her teeth and lowered her head. Her fingers twisted like claws. "You do not give orders here anymore!"

Ashley tipped a wine bottle back and wiped her mouth. "Back off, Irene. Have a drink with me!"

T-Bone cast a sideways glance at me. "She's not staying!"

"Babe," Ashley said, "Irene's my sister! We should all be able to sit down and share a drink!"

Irene's mouth stretched and widened. Black fur sprouted over her face.

"T-Bone!" I said. "You need to run!"

T-Bone turned to me, but I didn't take my eyes off Irene.

"Who the hell are you, anyway?" T-Bone asked.

I spoke aloud, but mostly to myself. "The killer couldn't have been Ashley. She's been performing here for weeks in front of tons of witnesses, a fool-proof alibi, and while her teeth might be deadly, they aren't large enough to make the kind of wounds I'd seen on that trucker's neck."

"What the hell are you talking about?" T-Bone asked.

Irene's mouth stretched into a giant grin as she landed on all fours. A deep vibration rose in her gut and erupted as a gravelly screech which made the hair's rise on my neck.

The tiger in the front room answered Irene's call with a quiet roar of its own.

I marveled at how close I had come to being like that truck driver in the morgue. If Irene hadn't needed my help finding her sister, I would have been a ride, or a place to stay, and then found dead in the morning.

Irene's clothes didn't tear, but somehow disappeared into her dark fur. She was half the size of the tiger, but sharp canines extended the length of her face, and there were no metal bars between us and them. Her sinewy body rippled across the room almost faster than I could follow.

I pulled old Harold back and drew my gun with quaking hands. The old man whipped out his cell phone and began dialing.

T-Bone finally saw what Irene had become. "What the—?"

Ashley moved between T-Bone and her sister. She stared into the face of the beast. "Stop it, Irene! You think you understand now because you gained some cool new ability! Because you can now *choose* to be an animal when you want to!"

The panther roared again with a mouth incapable of human speech.

"You don't know anything!" Ashley continued. "I'm like this all the time!"

T-Bone pulled a gun and took aim at the big cat.

Ashley grabbed his arm, ruining his shot. T-Bone shoved Ashley away, and her fingernails raked across his arm. She froze and covered her mouth, seeing the blood. "I'm sorry! It was an accident!"

He gritted his teeth and now took aim at Ashley.

"Stop!" I shouted. "You can't hurt her! Think about what you are doing! She's your meal ticket!"

T-Bone shook his head. "She's worthless now. No one will hire us after this!"

Irene reared up, snarling and lashing out with her paws. T-Bone turned his gun on the giant cat and let the bullets fly. Three shots dug into her dark fur before she let up.

Irene padded across the carpet, leaving a trail of bloody paw prints before crashing through the picture window. She winced with pain as she mounted the seven foot wall. Irene glanced back once and leapt away.

Ashley turned away from the window with tears in her eyes and looked down at T-Bone bleeding on the floor. "You were really going to shoot me?"

"I was just angry, baby. You know I love you!"

She shook her head and buried her face in her hands. I extended my arm and she leaned into me.

Two cops entered with drawn guns. We spent about forty minutes trying to explain to the police what had happened. They were convinced T-Bone and old Harold had been keeping a second big cat, and Slash was happy to corroborate that belief to cover for her sister.

Irene's bloody trail ended across the street. It was difficult to believe she might have survived three bullets at close range, but with no body, it remained a possibility, and that possibility comforted Ashley.

T-Bone kept trying to apologize to her, but when I left, Ashley left with me.

* * *

Ashley and I approached a three story building on a corner. No exterior signage identified the structure, and it was surrounded by a nine foot wall. We were still in the city, but things were much quieter here than near the strip, and after the crazy morning we'd had, the quiet was nice.

Ashley scrunched her nose up at the building.

"People at this shelter will help you." I looked at her. "Wearing that coat, you can pretty much blend in."

"I don't want to blend in anymore." She let the long coat drop to the pavement, revealing leopard-print tights and a tank top. "I used to be so jealous of my sister. *She* could blend in. This is who I am. There isn't anything wrong with the things I've done."

"Of course not! But you did all the work while other people took all the cash."

"T-Bone took care of the money, the contracts, finding places to stay, bought all the food. I'm not smart enough or strong enough to do all those things."

I shook my head. "You're selling yourself way short, Ashley. Once you start managing your own finances and find out how much money you were actually taking in, you might discover T-Bone was not as slick as he made you think."

"I knew he wasn't the smartest or the best, but he made me feel safe. Can you come inside with me?"

"I'm afraid not. No men allowed."

Her brow furrowed, and she frowned. "I don't suppose you have any Vicodin?"

"No. And I'm sure they don't allow drugs at the shelter either. T-Bone's pills made you easier to control."

"Just one to take the edge off wouldn't hurt."

I handed her my card. "Call me if you need anything or want to talk."

She examined the card. "Maybe I could come with you."

I wondered how the dogs would react to Ashley as a houseguest. "I wish you could. I really do, but my place is too small. Besides, you don't really want to stay with me. You're just afraid of being on your own. Are you sure you don't want to call your Aunt Sara?"

"Maybe someday, but not yet. You're right. I need some time on my own."

I nodded. "Keep in touch, Ashley. I want regular updates on how you are doing."

She turned to me, and her tail curled up playfully behind her. "Not Ashley. The name's Slash. And I'm going to be just fine."

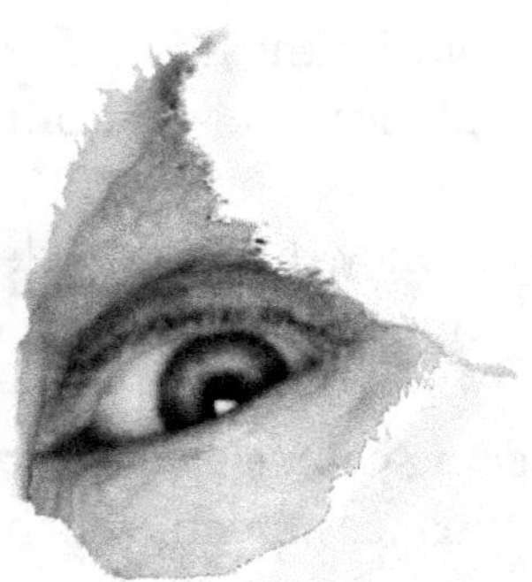

LEAVE THE BOOTS ON

How many times have I counted these same ceiling tiles? The persistent ringing in my ear makes it difficult to concentrate. If I could talk, I would tell my story, but all I can do is remember.

Particles floated in shafts of sunlight from the lone front window. I hadn't been in this musty bookstore for months, but I don't think a single book had been moved. How did they stay in business? I could have shopped for books online at home, but I needed to get out of the house. My home was a tomb, all shut up and covered in dust. Ever since Helen had broken my heart, I didn't see the point of cleaning.

A girl sat on a stool in the romance section. I had thought the place abandoned and never expected to see this beautiful vision. She wore a little hat with a black scarf tied into her hair, which was more orange than red or blonde. Her knees peeked out under her short skirt, barely suggesting the sweetness within. Just below her knees were long, black boots.

She looked up with wide, green eyes. "Can I help you?"

My face flushed. I must have been staring. "I'm sorry. I thought I was the only customer here."

"You aren't the only person who still reads books."

I still stared, but forced myself to smile. "There's something about a bookstore. Being able to browse and hold the books in your hands."

Her smile pierced the darkness around my heart. For the first time in months, I forgot about Helen.

The girl brought a book up to her nose and inhaled deeply. "I love the smell of them."

It was foolish, of course, to think a young woman like her would ever be interested in me. She looked to be barely in her twenties. I was at least fifteen years older than her. She dressed like Stevie Nicks. I wore pleated khakis and a pocket protector.

I searched for something to say. "You like... romance books?"

"No. I hate them. That's why I read them."

I was confused for a moment, then assumed she was making a joke at my expense.

"I love them because I hate them." She held the book up. "These things aren't real life. They are a fantasy version of reality, a better version." Her expression darkened. "Love isn't real. In real life, we are all just slaves to the chemicals in our brains."

"I'm surprised to hear something so cynical from someone so young." I kicked myself for inadvertently emphasizing our difference in age.

"I'm much older than I look," she said. "How old are you, anyway?"

"I'm..." There was no point in hiding it. "I'm thirty-nine."

"That's not so old." She showed me the spine of the book in her hand. "Have you read this author?"

"I'm not familiar with that particular author." I normally didn't read romance books.

Her expression brightened again. "She's the worst! Her characters are flat, and her stories are full of improbable coincidences." She closed her eyes and held the book to her breast. "I'm going to have to pick this one up."

I couldn't help but laugh.

"You think I'm silly?"

"Maybe a little," I said, "but a very charming sort of silly."

Her smile broadened. It seemed no trouble had ever blemished that young face.

Faces can lie.

"You seem to know a little about charm yourself." She took a marker out of her purse and, to my surprise, grabbed my hand. The felt tip tickled my skin. "Call me later. We should chill sometime."

"Sure," I said. After paying for her book, she gave one last look over her shoulder at me before exiting into the light. I stared at the closing door for a time before finally looking at my hand. Next to a series of numbers was the name *Honey.*

Out in the light of day, I took another look at the writing on my hand to make sure it wasn't some trick of the bookstore shadows. I smiled at the arching letters, then walked home and cleaned the house.

I transferred the number to a sheet of paper, but, even after showering, like a foolish schoolboy, I tried to preserve the fading writing on my hand.

Would I seem too eager if I called her that very night?

To hell with waiting. I dialed the digits, holding my finger over the last number for a moment before finally bringing it down. The phone went immediately to voicemail. There wasn't even a recording of her youthful voice.

"It's Carl," I said to no one. Did she even know my name? "From the bookstore," I added. "I was wondering if you wanted to... chill." *Chill.* The word sounded stupid from my lips.

I hung up and stared down at the phone.

It was seven o'clock. Helen, my ex, was probably finishing dinner about now. I could call her. We were on good terms, sort of. I mean, except for the fact that we weren't together anymore. She cared about me, in her way. I remembered Honey's comment about love and chemicals. I no longer provoked the chemical response that Helen called love.

I skipped dinner and went to bed early.

The phone woke me from a light sleep.

The sweet voice on the phone bounced with a playful rhythm. "Open mic night at the coffee shop across from the bookstore. Meet me there."

"Honey?"

She giggled. "How many girls were you expecting to call you tonight? I'll be there in ten minutes."

The clock read 10 pm. I had to be at work early the next morning. The rational thing to do would be to politely decline and arrange another time to meet.

"I'll see you there," I said.

I took another shower and brushed my teeth. I thought about shaving, but Honey might already be at the coffee shop.

The bookstore was just down the street, so I walked over. The closer I got, the more my heart thundered in my chest. The little coffee shop was full of artsy beautiful people. All conversation momentarily stopped when I walked in the door. I scanned the customers as I made for the back of the room, and they returned my look with a suspicious glare.

I didn't belong here, and Honey was nowhere to be seen. I found an unobtrusive spot in the back of the room.

Lithe arms grabbed me from behind.

"You came!" Honey's smile was warm and genuine.

"I said I would."

"Boys say lots of things."

Someone banged bongos while a woman rambled, trying to force words into a rhythm they didn't fit. One by one, poets expounded pretentiousness. Honey clapped and squealed after every one. The happiness on her face was worth losing sleep and sitting through trite poems.

Open mic was still going when Honey grabbed my arm and whispered, "You want to get out of here?"

"Sure. Where shall we go?"

"You live nearby?"

"Yeah."

She swung my hand back and forth playfully as we walked. It was unreal. Things like this didn't happen to me.

I was clumsy with the keys as I unlocked the door and was glad that I had cleaned the house that afternoon. The small two bedroom ranch wasn't the best house or the greatest neighborhood, but it was all mine, completely paid for. Helen would have preferred that I get a big place in the suburbs and spend the rest of my life in debt.

Honey circled the living room, examining the sparse contents. I spotted the photo of Helen on the mantel and attempted to grab it before Honey saw it, but she snatched it from my grasp.

"Who's this?" Honey asked. "Your wife?"

"No! She's just my— We're just—"

"It's okay if you're married."

I was speechless for a moment. Honey had certainly been flirting with me. Shouldn't it have mattered if I had a wife?

"She's my ex-girlfriend," I said.

Honey seemed to take sadistic pleasure in my discomfort. "Your ex? And you still keep her picture up?"

I was blowing it.

"It was a recent breakup," I said. "I don't know why I still have it out."

"She must be very important to you."

I took the picture and placed it face down on the mantel. "Helen and I are over. I guess I have a hard time letting go."

Honey studied me a moment. "You're telling the truth, aren't you?"

"Why would I lie?"

She put her arms around me and smiled. "You're sweet."

I just stared at her.

She closed her eyes and tilted her head. "Aren't you going to try to kiss me?"

I leaned in for a gentle kiss. She pulled my face into hers and sucked on my lips. For a moment, I feared she would gnaw them off. Her tongue shot into my mouth. There was a subtle tang to her kisses. At first, I didn't like the taste, but as I became more accustomed to it, I began to enjoy it. Kissing someone without that flavor would now be like watching a modern 3-D movie in flat black and white.

She led my hand to her thigh. I slid my fingers up as we kissed and found she wasn't wearing underwear. She fell back onto the couch and I kissed her thighs.

Her musk intoxicated me, drew my face forward like a magnet. I buried my nose inside her and worked it upward, licking as I did, lapping up her delicious juices.

All my troubles faded into nothing. My nose and lips became slick as I nudged her with my tongue and nibbled her puffy labia. I pressed my tongue against her and sucked gently. Her soft moans were briefly muted by her thighs pressing against my ears. Her black boots rested on my back.

The taste, the smell, the slick warmth drenching my face supercharged my body. I didn't have a ton of experience with women, but it wasn't like I had never performed oral sex before. It had never been like this.

No matter how close I was to her, it wasn't close enough. I would have crawled up inside her if I could.

I tugged on the zipper of her boot, but she grabbed my hand so hard it hurt.

"Leave the boots on," she said.

I didn't care about her boots at that moment. She pulled her blouse down, revealing plump peaches and tiny pink nipples. I let her pull my face back up to her juicy mouth and continued to kiss her while I undid my pants.

It ended much too quickly. I collapsed on top of her, trying to catch my breath. Honey tapped me on the shoulder, and I rolled off. She immediately pulled her blouse up and grabbed her purse.

I felt a strange apprehension. "Are you leaving already?"

"We should do this again sometime," she said.

The mere possibility of tasting her again made my anxiety subside a bit. "You don't have to leave yet," I said.

She narrowed her eyes. "Do you like me, Carl?"

I didn't know what to say. I barely knew her. "Maybe. I'd like to talk to you more."

Something in my answer pleased her. She beamed and gave me a warm kiss before she left. I stared at the closed door. It seemed like a dream, but that musky aroma still floated in the room and covered my face.

I had less than three hours before I needed to leave for work.

I lay in bed for a time and enjoyed the musk still adhering to my lips and nose. It made me sad that it wasn't as strong as the night before. I skipped showering and brushing my teeth, wanting to preserve the scent as long as I could.

I ambled into work twenty minutes late. My desk sat out in the open, right across from the boss's office. He glared at me, but I didn't care.

I looked over a stack of invoices and compared them to the orders I had placed the previous week. I was a procurement clerk for the OR at the local hospital. It wasn't glamorous, but it was a living. My tired mind drifted and I had to go over the invoices a second time.

I got an email from Helen. "Are you okay?" it read. "I haven't heard from you in a few days."

I stared at the computer screen. What was left to talk about? We were over. All Helen did when I called was complain about her job. I liked listening to her troubles, though. It made me feel I was still a part of her life in some small way.

My cell phone rang. I normally didn't answer my cell at work, but I checked the caller I.D.

It was Honey!

I checked to make sure no one was looking and kept my head low. "Honey?"

"I want to see you."

My heart leapt. "We can have dinner after work."

"I need to see you now."

"But I'm at work."

"I'm outside your place."

I didn't believe her at first. "You are at my house right now?"

"Mmm-hmm."

"But I—I'm at work now."

"But Carl, I might not be this wet later."

Her scent had faded from my lips. I needed more. "I'll be right there."

I crept into my boss's office with my head bowed. "Mr. Lowery, I'm not feeling well."

My boss furrowed his brow and peered over his glasses. "I should have known something was wrong when you showed up late. You're looking... disheveled. Do you need to see a doctor?"

"No! No. I'm sure I'll be fine after some sleep."

I had never played hooky before. I had to force myself not to charge gleefully from his office. My car ran over the curb as I parked in front of my house, but I left it as it was.

Honey smiled when I saw her on the front steps. She was leaning back, resting the weight of her shoulders on her hands. She shifted her knees as she stood, then bent over to pick up her purse. A black sundress hugged her round rump, and a breeze briefly revealed the bottom of a butt cheek. It would have aroused me before, but now I knew the nectar that hid within that fabric. I yearned for it. She still wore those tall, black boots.

It was difficult to unlock the door while kissing her at the same time. Her kisses were sweet, but they were nothing compared to what lay beneath that sundress.

She would have taken me on the couch again, but I led her to the bedroom. She pushed me onto the bed and shimmied the dress to the floor. She undid my pants and took me into her mouth. It was pleasant, but that's not what I wanted. I pulled her face to mine, kissing her before pushing her onto the bed.

I bit the zipper of one of her boots and tugged.

She closed her legs and grabbed her boot. "No!"

"Why?" Leaving them on last night had been fun, but today I wanted all of her.

"I'm just self conscious about me feet. That's all."

"You're being silly."

"I said no!" She slowly moved her leg aside, revealing her glistening flower. "Do you want me, or not?"

She knew that I did.

When we were done, I kissed her once on the lips and stared into her eyes. She was uncharacteristically bashful, and I smiled, clinging to her on the bed. Afternoon sun streamed in the window.

"What are you doing?" she asked.

"You mean... holding you?"

Honey shot into a sitting position and planted her boots on the floor. "I don't cuddle." She slipped the sundress over her shoulders.

I didn't want her to leave again. "Are you hungry? I could make some lunch."

She paused and peered at me over her shoulder. "What would you make?"

I tried to remember what I had in the kitchen. I hadn't been to the grocery in a while. "I could make... pancakes... sausage."

A smile crept across her face. "Breakfast for lunch. I like it."

Milky batter and sausages sizzled on the griddle. I used to make this for Helen when she spent the night.

Honey squealed, and I was afraid. I found her going through my records.

"Vinyl!" she said. "Nobody has vinyl anymore."

She pulled out *Rumours* by Fleetwood Mac. "This is the first record I ever bought! I played it every day until it got all scratched up."

"I've had that since I was a kid," I said. "My dad got it when it was brand new."

"So did I!" she said.

She wouldn't have been born when that album came out, but I didn't want to argue about something so trivial.

She put the record on the turntable and a scratchy rendition of 'Second Hand News' began to play. She bobbed her neck to the guitar. I was mesmerized by the sundress twirling around her as she spun. She grabbed me and whirled me around as well. I didn't really know how to dance, but I played along, and she giggled.

The smoke detector went off and I ran for the griddle.

Honey looked sad as she nibbled on two pancakes and a sausage patty. Before she was finished, she got up from the table.

"I need to go," she said.

"Are you going home?" I asked "To work?" I knew so little about her.

"It's all work, isn't it?"

"Huh?"

"Nothing."

She marched slowly toward the door with her head down.

"Are you sure you want to go?" I asked.

She forced a smile. "I have to."

"When will I see you again?"

"Is it me you want to see?"

"Well, yes. Who else?"

Her expression suddenly shifted into a mischievous grin. "We'll see."

"We'll see?"

"I'm a busy girl."

Terror gripped my heart. "Did I do something wrong?"

She studied me for a moment.

"I can change." It was a stupid thing for me to say. I barely knew this girl and didn't even know what I had done wrong.

"You will change," she said. "They all change. You will become the real Carl. This man I'm looking at right now, that's not you."

Honey slammed the door on her way out.

I ran out the door and called to her, but she was nowhere to be seen.

She was crazy. I was better off without her, but the thought of never tasting her again seemed worse than death. She had granted me a reprieve from my loneliness, but now I was worse than before.

I did the dishes and tried to watch television. My mind couldn't focus on anything I watched.

I thought about calling Helen, but I didn't know what to say to her. There was no way I could talk to her about Honey.

I went to bed early, exhausted, but instead of sleeping, I tossed and turned. I was cold, but my sheets were covered in sweat.

I needed Honey. I thought if I could just taste her one more time, I could get by.

My fingers shook when I dialed. It went straight to voicemail. My voice was a hoarse whisper. "Honey, it's Carl. I'm sorry about whatever I did. I want to see you. I need to see you." I tried to make it sound casual, but of course I was failing. "Call me whenever you get a chance."

I lay with the phone next to my face, hoping she would call back.

I walked into work forty-five minutes late. This was only the second time I had ever been late. Black circles sagged under my bloodshot eyes.

My hands shook as I logged into the computer and found a long list of items that needed ordered. I accidentally placed one order twice and had to cancel it.

My cell phone rang, and I checked the caller ID.

"Honey!" I said into the phone. "You called!"

She giggled. "Of course I called. Why wouldn't I?"

"I thought you were mad at me."

"Why would I be mad at you?"

"I don't know. The way you left—"

"I wasn't mad. I just had to go is all. I do have a life outside of you, you know."

I was afraid she would get mad again. "Of course you do! I know that."

"Do you still want to see me?" She asked.

"Yes!"

"I'm heading to your place now."

"Now? I'm at work."

"I'm a busy girl. I have time now."

My chest pulsed with rapid, shallow breaths, and sweat oozed from my pores. I needed a fix. "I'll be right there."

I wanted to run out without a word, but I had to say something. I needed this job. My house was paid off, but I still had taxes and electricity, phone, water, not to mention health insurance. I went into Mr. Lowery's office and tapped lightly on his open door.

He didn't look happy. "Close the door."

Mr. Lowery only asked people to close the door when he had something bad to say.

"Carl, you have always been a good employee—"

"Thank you, sir," I said, hoping he would hurry up. Honey was on her way to my house. It would be nice if I could take a shower before she arrived.

"Until now," he continued. "I've never seen you like this before. Did you know we almost had to cancel a surgery this morning because we ran out of stents?"

"What?" For a brief moment, I forgot about Honey. Hadn't I seen that invoice for stents on my desk yesterday? I wasn't sure. The thought of someone being prepped for surgery and then being told we didn't have the right supplies made me cringe.

"We were able to get some from North," Mr. Lowery said.

North was how we referred to our north side facility. I felt some relief, but the surgery would have still been delayed for at least a couple hours. That would affect the procedures scheduled around it, delays snowballing all day long, and it was my fault.

"You're not doing your job, Carl."

"I'm sorry, sir. I've not been feeling well."

"I can tell. I've talked to HR and they recommended I send you to see a counselor."

"A counselor? I don't need a—"

Mr. Lowery wrote a room number on a Post-it note. "They are waiting for you now."

"Now! I can't go now."

"They are in the building. It will only take thirty minutes. You will have plenty of time to finish your work when you're done."

Mr. Lowery gazed at me over his spectacles.

I took the Post-it. "Yes, sir," I said.

I stepped onto the elevator with a bowed head. The doors opened onto the second floor where the counseling center was. I stared at the open doors for a moment. They closed again, and I headed for the lobby.

I almost got into a car accident on my way out of the parking garage. Honey was already sitting on my front stoop when I arrived.

I knelt beside her and stared into her smiling face.

"What?" she asked.

I smiled and kissed her. This wasn't the passionate, desperate kiss either of us expected. This was a kiss of happy relief. I hadn't lost her. I took her to my room and laid her on the bed. I didn't fuck her. I worshiped her. My life was falling apart, but at that moment, her body was my world, and it was perfect.

She let me hold her and stroke her hair afterwards.

I awoke startled. I hadn't meant to doze off. I smiled when I realized Honey had fallen asleep as well. Her face was relaxed and content.

Those boots looked so uncomfortable. I decided to take them off and tuck her in. I pulled the zipper down slowly, careful not to wake her.

A few inches down from her knee, the skin of her calves was dry and flaky. I wondered if she ever took those boots off. A little further down, the skin became even more scaly, like pink reptile skin. It looked like a really bad case of psoriasis. It was no wonder she was so self-conscious.

I pulled the boot away, and three sharp toes grabbed my arm. I tried to pull away, but the grip tightened painfully and I feared the talons would cut my skin if I pulled too hard.

"Why?" Her eyes were full of hurt. "I told you I didn't like my feet! Why did you have to take off my boots?"

I couldn't believe what I was seeing. How did she manage to walk on those bird-like feet?

"You tricked me!" She said. "Making me comfortable. Letting me fall asleep!"

My eyes scanned up her leg to where the skin transitioned into the smooth, young flesh I was familiar with. My gaze reached her soft, wet slit, and I wanted her again.

Her foot still had hold of my arm, but Honey couldn't look me in the eyes. "These feet mark me as property. Through me, you are now property too."

"What? I'm no one's property!"

She snorted and released my arm. "Admit it. You don't even care. You've already forgotten about my feet. You don't care about me at all!" She spread her legs. "All you care about is this!"

With her legs spread wide, I could see the glistening gate to heaven. I could smell it, practically taste it. I needed it.

I moved toward her glistening, sweet love, but she rolled on her side. The sound of her quiet sobbing broke through my clouded mind.

Nirvana was right there, but out of reach.

"But I do care about you," I said. Did I? I had liked her before I experienced her, but now I was completely enthralled. Was that love? "Please," I said. "I need it."

She stopped sobbing and looked up at me with red, puffy eyes. "You will never have it again!"

My heart seemed to stop in my chest. I had to remind myself to continue breathing. "No! I'll die without it!"

She rolled her eyes. "You're no different than all the others. You won't die."

"I will. I'll die! I can't bear the thought of living the rest of my life never tasting it again! Never feeling it against my lips! I'd rather be dead!"

She rubbed her finger against herself and held the sticky sweetness in front of me. "There is only one way," she said. "You must do something for me first."

I darted my face forward, but she pulled her hand back.

"Something to prove your love," she said.

"Anything!" I said. There was nothing else in the world that mattered as much as her sweetness.

"Something horrible," she added.

* * *

Helen still kept the extra key under a particular rock behind some bushes by the back door. She had no reason to change. She had dumped me, broken my heart, but she had no reason to fear me. We were still friends, or at least acquaintances. It was no wonder she was startled when she flipped on the light and found me sitting in the easy chair.

She gasped and held her chest. "My God! Carl, what are you doing here?"

I didn't answer. I didn't even look at her. I had to do this.

"Carl?"

I finally brought the gun out. I didn't point it at her. I just held it.

"What is that?"

She knew what it was. The gun was surprisingly easy to obtain. I had never been in trouble before. There were no marks on my record.

Helen should have run. If she ran, I could shoot her in the back and be with Honey within the hour. Helen didn't run. She stood there looking at me.

I finally looked at her. I couldn't shoot her if I didn't look at her.

It was Helen, my Helen, with her bobbed brown hair and big eyes. Her favorite food was lasagna, but she didn't eat it because she was afraid it would make her breath smell bad. Helen watched an episode of *Buffy the Vampire Slayer* every night before going to bed, even though she had seen them all a hundred times before. There was a time when I would have done anything for her.

A vibration in my pocket startled me. I slowly whipped out my phone. It was a picture, a picture of Honey sucking on her finger. I knew where that finger had been, knew it was covered with sweet nectar. I needed her sweetness. I would rather die than live without it.

I pointed my gun at Helen.

Helen's eyes swelled and her face drained of color. "Carl, this isn't you! What happened?"

How could I explain? She would never understand. I had to do this. I needed that musky ambrosia.

My hand quaked.

"Carl?"

Helen's blue eyes looked so confused. She could not have expected this when she walked in the door. She was probably thinking about what to have for dinner, or preoccupied by problems at work.

I had loved Helen once. I still loved her, but she wasn't mine anymore.

I could never have Helen again, but I could have the sweetness if I completed this one simple task.

But then what? What else might Honey make me do? How would I get the sweetness if I was in jail? I swallowed, trying to moisten my dry mouth and get control of my breathing.

I had never hurt anyone before. I couldn't hurt someone I loved, but I couldn't live knowing that sweetness was out there and I would never taste it again.

I cocked the gun, and Helen's pupils contracted. I turned the gun around and opened my mouth.

I wasn't ready for the recoil, and my hand jerked as the thunder boomed. The ceiling and floor spun around me. Helen's screams were dwarfed by the painful ringing in my left ear.

My head jerked to a sudden stop.

* * *

The light was too bright. Water filled my right eye and the other didn't seem to work. I tried to swallow, but couldn't. There was something shoved down my throat. It forced air into me and then sucked it out again. I grimaced and tried to reach for my face, but my hand wouldn't respond.

I couldn't even kill myself right.

Who would even care that I was lying here? Certainly not Helen, not after what I had put her through.

A shadowy face came into view above me. "Carl?"

The voice filled me with fear, not the irrational passion it had once inspired. It was Honey's voice. The face was different, however, with rounder cheeks and a thicker neck. Lines around her eyes and mouth seemed frozen in a perpetual scowl. The black scarf looked silly in her thinning hair. This woman bore the scars of a hard life.

Tears formed in her eyes. "Thank you, Carl."

I wanted to ask, "For what?" But I had that tubing in my throat.

"You saved me," she said. "I don't know if you can understand my words, but I wanted you to know. You broke my curse. You were the first to ever refuse me... to refuse the thing I was. You are a good person, a genuinely good person."

My eye followed her around the bed.

"I can finally move on," she said. "Thanks to you."

She disappeared from view. I took some solace that my sacrifice had helped this stranger. Yes, she was a stranger. What did I really know about this woman called Honey?

I gazed up at the ceiling and began counting the tiles.

THE WORLDS OF MATTHEW BARRON

PARANORMAL MYSTERY

GRAPHIC NOVELS

SHORT STORIES

DYSTOPIAN

FANTASY

KID'S FICTION

AND MORE

AVAILABLE FROM

SUBMATTERPRESS.COM

ABOUT THE AUTHOR

Matthew Barron was raised by a dog in the cornfields of southern Indiana. His biological parents coaxed him back into the house with television and comic books. He still has a healthy distrust of humans, who are much scarier than anything in his stories.

In addition to two indispensable creative writing classes, Matthew got a degree in Clinical Laboratory Science from Indiana State University and became a medical technologist in Indianapolis, Indiana.

Matthew's diverse stories have appeared in several magazines and anthologies such as *Generation X-ed, And the Dead Shall Sleep No More, Ill-Considered Expeditions,* and many more. In addition to his prose books and short stories, he's produced two of his plays—*I'm Not Gay* (2015) and *Phantom of Fountain Square* (2019)—and released three graphic novels: *Temple of Secrets, The Brute: Chasing Shadows* and *Harmony Unbound.* In 2020 he started the Jack Mahler paranormal mystery series with *Waking Terror,* and in 2024 he finally collected 30 years worth of short stories in *Dissonant Dreams.*

His sword sorcery book *Valora,* dystopian novella *Secular City Limits,* and children's book *The Lonely Princess* are also available.

For more information, visit
matthewbarron.com
or
submatterpress.com

www.ingramcontent.com/pod-product-compliance
Lightning Source LLC
Chambersburg PA
CBHW071946190726
48293CB00004B/1379